One day soon she was going to have to grow a backbone when it came to Nicholas, or they were in for a very rocky ride as he grew up.

It was just that she needed to lavish him with love, show him how much he mattered to her. She would not become her parents—throwing money at every situation when more often than not a hug would suffice. No. Nicholas would always know how much she cared about him. *Always.*

A big, warm and strong hand cupped her chin, tilted her head back so that she stared into Jackson's green gaze.

'Jess? Where have you gone? Something up?'

With an abrupt shake of her head she stepped away from that hand and those all-seeing eyes. It would be too easy to lean into him, burden him with her problems. That would certainly put the kibosh on getting to know him better. He'd suddenly have so much to do she'd not even see his delectable butt departing for all the dust he'd raise on the way out. She mightn't be sophisticated but she knew the rules. She'd invented some of them.

Keep it simple.

Do not get too close.

Dear Reader

Golden Bay is one of New Zealand's gems. There's only one road in, but it's well worth the effort to go there. I've spent a few summer holidays staying at one of the beaches there, enjoying the fishing, swimming and just relaxing. I also have family living there, and I attended a wonderful wedding on their lawn which gave me ideas leading to these stories.

Sasha and Grady, Jessica and Jackson—all have family connections and history from when they were teenagers. But people have to leave the bay area if they want to attend university, and not everyone comes back. Of course I had to bring these four back. I hope you enjoy their ensuing relationships and how they find love again.

Cheers!

Sue MacKay

PS I'd love to hear from you at sue.mackay56@yahoo.com or visit me on www.suemackay.co.nz

The first story in Sue MacKay's
***Doctors to Daddies* duet**

A FATHER FOR HER BABY

**is also available this month
from Mills & Boon® Medical Romance™**

THE
MIDWIFE'S SON

BY
SUE MacKAY

Published in Great Britain 2014
by Mills & Boon, an imprint of Harlequin (UK) Limited,
Eton House, 18-24 Paradise Road, Richmond, Surrey, TW9 1SR

© 2014 Sue MacKay

ISBN: 978 0 263 24381 9

Harlequin (UK) Limited's policy is to use papers that are natural,
renewable and made from wood grown in
sustainable forests. The logging and manufacturing processes conform
to the legal environmental regulations of the country of origin.

Printed and bound in Great Britain
by CPI Antony Rowe, Chippenham, Wiltshire

With a background of working in medical laboratories and a love of the romance genre, it is no surprise that **Sue MacKay** writes Mills & Boon® Medical Romance™ stories. An avid reader all her life, she wrote her first story at age eight—about a prince, of course. She lives with her own hero in the beautiful Marlborough Sounds, at the top of New Zealand's South Island, where she indulges her passions for the outdoors, the sea and cycling.

Recent titles by Sue MacKay:

FROM DUTY TO DADDY
THE GIFT OF A CHILD
YOU, ME AND A FAMILY
CHRISTMAS WITH DR DELICIOUS
EVERY BOY'S DREAM DAD
THE DANGERS OF DATING YOUR BOSS
SURGEON IN A WEDDING DRESS
RETURN OF THE MAVERICK
PLAYBOY DOCTOR TO DOTING DAD
THEIR MARRIAGE MIRACLE

These books are also available in eBook format from www.millsandboon.co.uk

Dedication

Thanks very much to Kate Vida for her medical help.
Any mistakes are mine.
And to Deidre and Angela, because I can.

Praise for
Sue MacKay:

'An emotional drama full of powerful feelings and
emotions. An immensely satisfying read on all
counts—a wonderfully human story which will leave
the reader moved. I look forward to reading more
books by this author in the future.'
—*Contemporary Romance Reviews* on
THE GIFT OF A CHILD

'The first book in this duet, THE GIFT OF A CHILD
by Sue MacKay, is a deeply emotional, heart-rending
story that will make you smile and make you cry.
I truly recommend it—and don't miss the second book:
the story about Max.'
—*HarlequinJunkie.com*

'What a great book. I loved it. I did not want it to end.
This is one book not to miss.'
—*GoodReads.com* on
THE GIFT OF A CHILD

CHAPTER ONE

JESSICA BAXTER STARED at the champagne glass twirling between her thumb and forefinger. It was empty. Again. How had that happened? Best fill it up. She reached for the bottle nestled in ice in the silver bucket beside her.

'You planning on drinking that whole bottle all by yourself?' The groomsman sat down beside her, his steady green gaze fixed on her. Eyes so similar to his sister Sasha's, yet far more dramatic. The way they were sizing her up at this moment sent shivers of anticipation through her. But it was more likely she had whipped cream and strawberry compote on her nose rather than anything earth-shatteringly sensual going on.

Her finger shook as she wiped the top of her nose. Nope. All clear of dessert. So what was fascinating Jackson Wilson so much that his head seemed to have locked into position and his eyes forgotten how to move? Maybe if she answered him he'd get moving again.

So she told him, 'Yes.' Every last drop.

'Then I'll have to get my own bottle. Shame to have to move, though.' Jackson smiled at her, long and slow, making her feel as though she was the only person in the marquee. The only woman at least.

Which was blatantly untrue. Apart from Sasha, who was looking absolutely fabulous in a cream silk wed-

ding gown, there had to be half the female population
of Golden Bay in this marquee. Hadn't Sasha said she
wanted a small wedding? Define small. Jess looked at
the bottle in her hand. Had she drunk too much? Not yet.
'This has to be the best champagne I've ever tasted. Your
father went all out.'

'Can't argue with that.'

She wasn't looking for an argument. Her mouth curved
upwards. Just some more champagne. The bubbles sped
to the surface as she refilled her glass. The sight was
enough to turn a girl on. If you were the kind that got
turned on easily. Which she definitely wasn't. Her eyes
cruised sideways, spied Jackson's legs stretched far under
the table, and stilled. Well-toned thighs shaped his black
evening trousers to perfection. Her tongue stuck to the
top of her mouth, her skin warmed, and somewhere
below her waist she felt long-forgotten sensations of desire. Maybe she was that kind of girl after all.

She lifted the bottle in Jackson's direction. 'Got a
glass?'

'Of course.' He presented one with a flourish. 'I never
go unprepared.' That gaze had returned, stuck on her, apparently taking in every detail of her face.

She paused halfway through filling his glass, raising
a well-styled eyebrow. 'Has my mascara run or something?'

Jackson shook his head. 'Nope.'

Spinach in my teeth? Except spinach hadn't featured
on the wedding dinner menu. So what was he looking
at? Looking for? Jackson Wilson had never taken much
notice of her before. They hadn't even liked each other
much during the two years she had gone to school here;
both had been too busy trying to steal the limelight.

The last time she'd seen him had been at their school

graduation party. Thirteen years ago. He'd been the guy every girl had wanted to date. She'd been the girl everybody had invited to their parties because she could supply anything money could buy. They'd never hooked up.

'Hey, stop.' He said it quietly, in that bone-melting voice of his. 'My glass runneth over.'

'What?' Eek. Bad move. She'd been so distracted she'd started pouring again without realising. So unlike her. Worse, he knew exactly what she was distracted by—him. Suck it up, and get over him. He's a minor diversion.

Jackson raised his fingers to his mouth and lapped up the champagne. Had he heard her telling herself to suck it up? She shivered deliciously. The gesture was done so naturally that she had to presume Jackson hadn't meant it as a sexual come-on. But, then, why would it be? She'd be the last female on earth he'd come on to. They probably still wouldn't get on very well; she was a solo mum, he was used to glamorous, sexy ladies who didn't sport stretch marks on their tummies.

Wait up. He'd only been back in Golden Bay for five days and before today she'd only seen him at the wedding rehearsal. She might have that completely wrong. She was open to having her opinion changed. He didn't look so full of himself any more. No, rather world-weary and sad, if anything.

Then Jackson seemed to shake himself and sit up straighter. Lifting his glass carefully, he sipped until the level dropped to a safe place, before clinking the rim of the glass with hers. 'To the happy couple.'

'To Sasha and Grady.' She should be looking for her friends as they danced on the temporary floor in the centre of the marquee, but for the life of her she couldn't drag her attention away from Jackson. When had he got so handsome? Like so handsome she wanted to strip him naked. Back at school, she'd never been as enthralled as all the other girls, but maybe she'd missed something. His body was tall and lean. His face had a chiselled look, a strong jawline and the most disconcerting eyes that seemed to see everything while giving nothing away.

'Has my mascara run?' he quipped.

Her face blazed. Caught. Why was that any different from him scrutinising her? It wasn't, but she never normally took the time to look a guy over so thoroughly. She usually wasn't interested. 'Yes.'

'Wonderful. My macho image is shattered.' His deep chuckle caught her off balance.

That made her study him even closer. There were deep lines on either side of that delectable mouth. More of them at the corners of those eyes that remained fixed on her. What had caused those lines? To avoid getting caught in his gaze she glanced at his hair, dark brown with a few light strands showing in the overhead lights. Grey, yet not grey. She glanced back to those eyes. 'You look exhausted.'

Jackson blinked, tipped his head back to stare at the top of the marquee. His mouth had tightened, instantly making Jessica regret her words. There was no way she wanted to upset him; she didn't want him to think she was probing, being nosey. 'Sorry. I take that back.' She sipped her champagne, the glass unexpectedly trembling in her hand.

'I am totally beat.'

Phew. Still talking. 'Jet-lag?' She supposed it was a longish haul from Hong Kong.

'Nah. Life.' His hand groped on the tabletop for his drink.

'Here.' She pushed it into his fingers.

'Thanks.' Sitting straighter, he took a deep taste of the nectar. 'You're right. This is superb.'

Again she wondered what hiccups there had been in his life to make him look so shattered. From what she knew, he worked as an emergency specialist in a huge hospital in Hong Kong. That would keep him busy, but many specialists put in the long hours and didn't end up looking as jaded as Jackson did right now. He'd be earning big money and no doubt had a fancy apartment and housekeeper, along with the to-die-for car and a string of women to ride alongside him. Maybe one of those women had caused a ripple in his otherwise perfect life? 'Why Hong Kong?'

'To live? I did part of my internship there and was offered a position in the emergency department for when I qualified.' Now he stared into his glass, seeming to see more than just the bubbles rising to the top. 'Hong Kong was exciting, buzzing with people, and completely different from Golden Bay. It was like starting a whole new life, unhindered by the past.'

'You sound like you hated it here.' What had happened to make him want to head offshore?

'I did at times.' Draining the glass, he reached for the bottle, peered at it. 'We need another one. Be right back.'

Jess watched Jackson stride around the edge of the dance floor, ignoring the women who tried to entice him to dance with them. So he was determined to sit with her for a while and share a drink. Why? Why her of all the people here? There had to be plenty of family and friends he knew from growing up in Takaka, people he'd want to catch up with. Come to think of it, she hadn't noticed him being very sociable with anyone in particular all day. Not that he'd been rude, just remote. Interesting. There must be more to this man than she knew.

Was she a safe bet, unlikely to molest him because she sat alone, not leaping up to shake and gyrate to the music?

Well, he'd got that right. She didn't come on to men any more. Not since the last one had made her pregnant and then tossed 'Don't send photos' over his shoulder on the way out, heading about as far north as earth went.

The sound of a cork popping as Jackson returned was like music to her ears. 'What is it about champagne that's so special?' she asked, as he deftly topped up her glass. 'Is it the buzz on the tongue?'

'That, the flavour and the fact that champagne goes with celebrations. Good things, not bad.' Somehow, when he sat back down, his chair had shifted closer to hers.

'I guess you're right.' Goose-bumps prickled her skin and she had to force herself not to lean close enough to rub against his arm. Bubbles tickled her nose when she sipped her drink and she giggled. Oops. Better go easy on this stuff. Then again, why not let her hair down and have a good time? It had been for ever since she'd done that.

'Of course I'm right.' He smiled, slowly widening his mouth and curving those delectable lips upwards, waking up the butterflies in her stomach and sending them on a merry dance. Then he said, 'That shade of orange really suits your brown eyes and fair hair.'

'Orange? Are you colour blind, or what? Your sister would have a heart attack if she heard you say that. It's apricot.' She fingered the satin of her dress. Being bridesmaid for Sasha had been an honour. It spoke of their growing friendship and being there for each other. One of the best things about returning home to Golden Bay had been getting to know Sasha, whom previously she'd only thought of as the girl about the bay who was younger and wilder than her. But that had been then. Nowadays they both were so tame it was embarrassing.

Jackson shrugged. 'Orange, apricot, whatever. You should wear it all the time.'

'I'll remember that.'

'Do you want to dance?'

What? Where had that come from? Dancing had nothing to do with dress colours. 'No, thanks.'

'Good. I'm hopeless at dancing. Always feel like a puppy on drugs.' His smile was self-deprecating.

'Then why did you ask?' She seemed to remember him gyrating around the floor at school dances.

'Thought you might want to.' He chuckled again. Deep and sexy.

'Luckily for you I'm not into dancing either.' She could get addicted to that chuckle. It sent heat zipping through her, warming her toes, her tummy, her sex. Once more her cheeks blazed, when they'd only just cooled down after the last time. What was going on here? She never blushed. It must be the drink. She stared at her glass belligerently and tried to push it aside, but couldn't. Not when she was letting her hair down for the first time in years and enjoying a drink or three. Nicholas was staying with his little friend, Bobby, just down the road at Pohara Beach. Tonight was hers to make the most of, mummyhood on hold for a few hours. Tomorrow reality would kick back in and she'd pick up the reins again. Not that she ever really let them go. But for one day and night it was great to be able to stop worrying.

'How old is your little boy?'

So mindreading was one of Jackson's talents. 'He's four and a handful. A gorgeous, adorable handful who keeps me on my toes nonstop.' He'd looked so cute at the marriage ceremony in his long trousers and white shirt.

'What happened to his dad?'

This man was blunt. 'Which rumour did you hear?' she asked, as she contemplated how much to tell.

'That he was a soldier on secondment who didn't take

you with him when he left. That he was the married CEO of a big company who liked beautiful young women on his arm.' Jackson drank some more champagne. Was that what had made him suddenly so talkative? 'That he was an alien visiting from Mars for a week.'

Her growing anger evaporated instantly and she dredged up a smile. 'Guess you know you're home when everyone starts making up stories about you.'

'Which is why I hightailed it out of here the day after I finished school.'

'Really?' Jess could feel her eyebrows lifting and brought them under control. How much would he tell her?

The steady green gaze locking onto her lightened. 'Really. I hated it that I couldn't sneeze without someone telling me I'd done something wrong.'

Not much at all. Memories niggled of a rumour about Jackson and a pregnant girl, something to do with a set-up. 'It's like that, isn't it? Claustrophobic.' She shuffled around on her chair, all the better to study him again. 'But there's also security in that.'

'You haven't told me which story is true. I'm guessing none of them.'

Persistent man. Or was he just shifting the focus off himself? She didn't talk about Nicholas's father. Not a lot of point. 'I prefer the alien one.'

He nodded. 'Fair enough.'

That's it? He wasn't going to push harder for information? Most people wouldn't care that the subject had nothing to do with them. She could get to like Jackson Wilson. Really like him. 'How long are you home for?'

'Almost three months.'

Her eyebrows were on the move upwards again. Three months? That seemed a long time when Sasha had mentioned this was his first visit in thirteen years. Of course, his mother had MS now. And there was Sasha's baby girl, Melanie, to get to know. 'Amazing how weddings bring people together from all corners of the world.'

'You're fishing.' He grinned at her.

'Am I catching anything?' She grinned straight back.

His grin faded. His focus fixed on her. Again. She was getting used to his intense moods. 'I need a break. A long one.' He stretched those fascinating legs further under the table and crossed them at the ankles. 'And now you're going to ask why.'

Putting all the innocence she could muster into her gaze, she tapped her sternum. 'Me? No way.' Then, unable to hold that look, she grinned again. 'If you don't tell me I'll have to torture you.'

His mouth curved upwards as his tongue slicked over his bottom lip. 'Interesting.'

Idiot. She'd walked into that one. Now he'd make some smutty comment and ruin the easy camaraderie between them. 'Um, forget I said that.'

'Forgotten.' Did he add, 'Unfortunately,' under his breath?

She so wasn't into leather and handcuffs, or whips and ice. At least she hadn't been. Her mouth twitched. Maybe she should head home now, before the champagne made her say more things she shouldn't.

Where were Sasha and Grady? Right in the centre of the floor, still dancing, wrapped around each other as though they were the only people there. A sudden, deep envy gripped her, chilled her despite the summer heat.

She wanted what they had. Wanted a man who loved her more than anything, anyone else. Who'd put her first. A man to curl up against at night, to laugh and cry with. A man like— Her eyes swivelled in her head, away from the dance floor right to the man beside her. A man like Jackson? No. For starters, he was her best friend's brother. Then there was the fact he was only home for a few months. Add his sophistication and Jackson was so not right for her.

Hold that thought. Focus on it. Believe it. Remember how she'd thought Nicholas's father would give her all those things, only to be shown just how wrong she'd been. Instead, she'd found a man incapable of commitment, even to his wife back in the States. A wife she hadn't had a clue about.

Unfortunately for her, right now, all the reasons for not getting involved with Jackson seemed to have no substance at all.

CHAPTER TWO

JACKSON WATCHED JESSICA. Her brown eyes lightened to fudge and darkened to burnt coffee depending on her emotion, flicking back and forth so fast sometimes she must give herself a headache. Talk about an enigma. One moment all shy and unsure of herself, the next flipping a sassy comment at him like she wanted him. Which was the real Jess Baxter?

Suddenly the months looming ahead didn't seem so long and depressing. Instead, they were beginning to look interesting. Could he spend some time with Jessica and get to know her? Have some light-hearted fun for a while and find the real woman behind that sharp mind and sad face? He enjoyed puzzles, but right now he didn't even know where to begin solving this one. They were hitting it off fine. There might be some fun to be had here.

But— Yeah, there was always a but. He didn't want involvement. Especially not with a woman who'd require him to stay on at the end of those months, to become a permanent resident in the one place that he'd decided before he'd turned fifteen wasn't right for him. Too small, too parochial. Too close and personal. Nasty, even. He'd never forget the gut-squeezing, debilitating hurt and anger when Miriam Blackburn had accused him of getting her pregnant. He'd only ever kissed her once.

No wonder big cities held more attraction. Easy to lose himself, to avoid the piranhas.

From the little Sasha had told him, he understood that Jessica had come home permanently. That she'd begun mending bridges with the people she wrongly believed she'd hurt years ago. Apparently she wanted her son to grow up here, where he'd be safe and looked out for. There was no arguing with that sentiment.

He definitely wasn't looking for commitment in any way, shape or form. Commitment might drag him back to the place he'd spent so long avoiding. He wasn't outright avoiding women. But Jessica wasn't like his usual type of woman. Those were sophisticated and well aware of how to have a good time without hanging around the next day. Women who didn't get under his skin or tug at his heartstrings.

Jessica would want more of him than an exciting time. She'd want the whole package. Settle down, have more babies, find a house and car suitable for those children. *And what was so awful about that?* No idea, except it was the complete opposite from what he wanted.

Back up. He mustn't forget why he'd decided to stay on after his sister's wedding. He needed to spend time with his family, to help Mum and Dad as they came to terms with the multiple sclerosis that had hit Mum like a sledgehammer. He'd also like to get to know his niece. Melanie was so cute and, at three months old, had wound him round her little finger. Already, memories of her smile, her cry, her sweet face were piling up in his head to take back with him to Hong Kong.

Then there was the small issue of needing to rest and recoup his energy, to find the drive to continue his work in Hong Kong and keep his promise to his dead colleague. That motivation had been slipping away over the last year, like fine grain through a sieve. The cata-strophic events of last month had really put the lid on his enthusiasm for his work. But a promise was a promise. No going back on it.

Clink. 'Drink up.' Jessica was tapping her glass against his again.

Yeah, drink up and forget everything that had hap-pened in the past month. Let it go for a few hours and have some uncomplicated fun. 'Cheers,' he replied, and drained his glass. Picking up the bottle, he asked, 'More?'

He saw her hesitating between yes and no, her eyes doing that light then dark thing. He made up her mind for her. 'Here, can't let this go to waste.' When he'd filled both glasses, he lifted them and handed over hers, tak-ing care not to touch her fingers as they wound around the glass stem. That would be fire on ice. 'To weddings and families and friends.'

She nodded, sipped, and ramped up his libido as she savoured the sparkling wine, her tongue licking slowly over her lips, searching for every last taste. So much for avoiding contact. She could heat him up without a touch. That mouth... He shook his head. He would not think about her champagne-flavoured lips on his skin. Or her long, slim body under his as he plunged into her. While he lost himself for a few bliss-filled moments. Hours, even.

She was talking, her words sounding as though she was underwater.

Focus, man. Listen to Jess. Ignore your lust-dazed brain. 'What did you just say?'

'Looks like the happy couple are on the move.' Her eyes followed his sister and new brother-in-law as they did the rounds of their guests, hugging and kissing and chatting.

'You and Sasha never used to be mates.'

Jess had been the girl with the rich parents who had bought her anything and everything she could ever have wanted. Yet she'd never seemed genuinely, completely happy, always looking for more. Definitely a party girl, always in the thick of anything going down in Takaka, but at the same time she'd seemed removed from everyone. Like a child looking out the lolly-shop window at the kids gazing in at the sweet treats.

Yet she'd had more than the rest of them put together, having spent most of her childhood apparently travelling to weird and wonderful places. Hadn't she had love? Had that been her problem? It would go a long way to explaining why she'd always bought her pals anything they'd hankered after. Perhaps she had been buying affection and friendship. Talk about sad.

Right now a big smile lit up her face, lightened her eyes. 'The day Sasha walked into the medical centre to start her job we just clicked. Guess that amongst our past friends we're the odd ones out, having left and come back. We've tasted the world, know what life's like on the other side of Takaka Hill, and returned. Though Sasha's done a lot more than I have when it comes to our careers.'

'You didn't work overseas?'

'Nope. I'd travelled a lot with my parents when I was a child. The idea of working in another country didn't appeal. Auckland was enough for me.'

'Are your parents still living here?'

Coffee-colour eyes. And her teeth nibbled at her bottom lip. 'Not often.'

He recognised a stop sign when he saw one. 'Here comes the happy couple.' Jackson stood, placed a hand on Jessica's elbow and pulled her up to tuck her in beside him. Her warm length felt good against his body. The side of her thigh rubbed against his, her elbow nudged his ribs. A perfume that reminded him of Mum's citrus grove teased his nostrils. Her hair, all fancy curls with orange ribbons woven through, tickled his chin when he lowered his head.

I want her. Like, really want her. Not just a five-minute quickie behind the shed either.

Surprise ricocheted through him and he felt his muscles tighten. All his muscles. Especially below his belt. Why was he surprised? Hadn't this need been growing all evening? Against him Jess jerked, looked up with a big question in those pull-you-in eyes.

Don't move. Hold your breath and wish away your out-of-left-field reaction to her before she catches on. Because otherwise she's going to empty what's left in that champagne bottle over your head.

His stomach dropped in time with her chin as she glanced down, over his chest to his waist, and on down. His breath caught somewhere between his lungs and his mouth. She'd have to be blind not to see his boner.

Her head lifted. Her gaze locked onto his. She clearly wasn't blind. Those brown pools were filled with comprehension. Raising herself up on tiptoe, she leaned close and whispered, 'Your place or mine?'

'Yours.' Definitely not his. He was currently staying at his parents' house.

Her hand slipped into his and she tugged him off balance. 'What are we waiting for?'

'I have no idea.' So now he was in the flirty corner of the Jessica puzzle. Fine by him. He'd look into the shy corner another day.

Sasha and Grady stepped in front of them. 'Hey, you two. In a hurry to leave?' Sasha asked, with an annoying twinkle in her eyes. 'Without saying goodbye?'

Jackson removed his hand from Jessica's and carefully hugged his sister. 'You look beautiful, sis. No wonder Grady hasn't moved more than two centimetres away from you all day.'

Then he slapped Grady on the back and stepped away to watch the two women hugging tightly. They'd got so close. Like they shared everything. A small knot of longing tightened in his gut. He wanted that, too. No, he wanted what his sister and Grady had. Wanted to be able to talk about what had happened last month, share his fear and apprehensions, even the promise that hung over him. He would like to know there was someone special to look forward to going home to every night, someone who wasn't the housekeeper.

Jessica? Maybe, maybe not. Though so far tonight she'd been totally in tune with him, not pushing for answers to questions he refused to give, understanding when he wanted to talk and when he didn't. Knowing how his body reacted to hers.

Which reminded him. Weren't they going somewhere? In a damned hurry, too?

'See you two tomorrow,' he told Grady, and grabbed for Jess's hand. He whispered, 'We're out of here.'

And received a big, knowing smile in return. 'Sure are, Doctor.'

As they passed the bar he swiped a bottle of champagne and tucked it under his free arm. 'Neither of us is driving tonight. Let's hope one of those vans Dad organised for transporting inebriated guests home is available.' Like right this minute. Hanging around waiting for a ride and being forced to listen while other guests talked and laughed in their ears would be a passionkiller for sure. Though the beach was a short walk through the flaxes if need be.

They were in luck. The beach could wait for another night. Two vans were lined up so they snaffled one and ten long, tension-filled minutes later Jess was unlocking her front door.

She didn't bother with lights. 'There's enough light from the full moon to see what we need to see. The rest we can do by touch.' Her laughter was soft and warm, touching him in a way none of the sophisticated women he'd bedded had. Was this shy Jessica? Or fun Jessica?

'Where are the glasses?' he asked as he popped the cork on the champagne.

'Come with me.' She reached for his hand. Being tugged through the small house by this gorgeous woman with only moonlight to see by was a breathtaking experience, heightening his senses—and his growing need for her.

Jess's slim outline with those just-right curves outlined by her gown hardened him further. Her backside shaped the fabric to perfection, her hips flared the almost skin-tight skirt subtly. 'How are you going to get out of that dress?'

They'd reached the kitchen, where she removed two champagne glasses from a cupboard and handed them to him. Her mouth curved into a delicious, cat-like smile. 'That's your job.'

Give me strength. He wouldn't last the distance. 'Right.'

Just then she turned, pressed up against him, her thighs pushing against his, her lush breasts squashed against the hard wall of his chest. Her hands slid around his neck and pulled his head down so her mouth covered his. His pulse went from normal to a thousand in a flash. Wrapping his free arm around her, he hauled her close, so close her lower belly covered his reaction to her, smothered it, warmed it.

'Gawd, Jess. Keep this up and we'll be over before we've started.'

Her mouth pulled back barely enough for her to reply, 'And your problem is?'

'Why did we stop to get glasses?' His lips claimed hers again. She tasted sweet, exciting, sexy. She tasted of what he so badly needed right now. Of freedom and oblivion. Of recovery.

Somehow she began stepping backwards, taking him with her, not breaking their kiss at all, not removing those breasts from his chest. Back, back, until they made it into another room. Thank goodness there was a bed. A big bed. His knees were turning to something akin to badly set jelly as desire soared through him. He was about to explode and that was only under the ministrations of her mouth on his. He lifted his head. 'Turn around so I can free you.'

She spun so quickly she almost lost her balance. 'Oops. I need to slow down.'

'Really?' Jackson reached for her zip. Idiot. He still held the champagne bottle and glasses in one hand. Oh, so carefully he placed them on the bedside table. He had completely lost where he was. All he knew was that Jess stood before him and that he wanted her like he'd never wanted a woman before. He was desperate for her. But first he needed her naked. He concentrated on pulling the zip down with fingers that refused to stop trembling. Desire vibrated through him, everywhere, not just his fingers, like this was totally new to him.

It was hard to understand. He hadn't been living in a monastery. Far from it. There'd been a steady stream of women through his bedroom most of his adult life. Yet now he was losing control like the teenager he'd been last time he'd lived in this place, wanting desperately to bury himself inside Jessica Baxter.

'Jackson. What's going on back there?'

'The zip's caught.' Idiot. Couldn't even undo a simple zip. 'Hang on.'

She giggled. 'Hang on? Whatever you want.' Her hand slid behind her and found him. Her fingers slid up and down his covered erection, while the other hand worked his fly, which she obviously had no difficulty with. His trousers were suddenly around his ankles. 'I'm trying to get a hold.'

'Jess, I'll never get you out of this dress if you keep doing that.' And I'll come before I get my boxers down as far as my knees.

Instantly she stilled, her body tense, but he could feel her heat, knew her pulse was working overtime by the way her breasts rose and fell rapidly. She sucked her stomach in so tight it must've hurt. 'Well?'

'Thank you,' he muttered, as he tugged downwards. 'At last.' He slid his hands inside the soft fabric, his fingers sliding over her hot skin, across her back to her waist, round to her stomach and up to cup those luscious breasts. Free breasts. 'You haven't got a bra on.'

'Would've ruined the look.' She wriggled her butt against him. Sucked in her breath. 'Jackson, your thumbs are sending me over the edge to some place I've never been.'

Music to his ears. 'That's nothing to the storm your hand's stirring up.' His erection felt large, hard, throbbing and ready to explode.

She leant forward, teasing him with her rear end as she shrugged her upper body out of the dress and let it fall to her feet. Then she stepped out of the puddle of orange fabric and turned to face him. Insecurity and sass warred on her face, vied for supremacy. 'We haven't kissed. Not once.'

Jackson wasn't sure he'd make it through a kiss. But that uncertainty blinked out at him from her dark eyes and he hauled on the brakes, pulled his hands from where they'd fallen to her waist, and encircled her with his arms. He so wanted to get this right for her. For him. Hell, he knew it would be great for him, but if Jessica wanted a kiss then she'd get one she'd never forget. When his mouth covered hers he couldn't believe he hadn't done this earlier. She tasted of champagne and the promise of hot sex. She also tasted of honest-to-goodness, trustworthy woman with a lot to offer and something to take.

When she pushed her tongue into his mouth to tangle with his he thought he'd died and gone to heaven. His jelly knees melted and they tipped onto the bed, neither breaking their hold on the other. As they rolled and sprawled he continued to devour her mouth. Until now he'd thought kissing highly overrated, but this moment had rewritten his ideas. Kissing Jess went so far off the scale he might never come back to earth.

Then her hand found him again. Forget kissing. His lungs seemed to fold in on themselves as all the air hissed over his teeth. Forget everything. Absolutely everything.

Pulling her mouth away, Jess said, 'You mentioned always being prepared for anything. I guess that means you've got a condom or two in your pocket.'

He froze. Swore under his breath. No. He'd been going to his sister's wedding, had not expected to be bedding a hot bridesmaid.

Hot, shaky laughter filled the room. 'You owe me, buster. Top drawer by the bed. They're probably out of date but better than nothing.'

Within moments she had him covered and her hand was back on him, heat rolling through every cell of his body.

He had to touch her. But suddenly he was on his back and Jess was straddling him. Before he'd caught up with her she was sliding over him, beginning to ride him. His hands gripped her thighs, his thumbs slipped over her wet heat to find her core. She instantly bucked and for a moment she lost the rhythm.

But not for long. Her recovery was swift. This woman had to be something else. He kept the pressure on as he rubbed across her wetness.

Above him Jessica let out a long groan and squeezed tight around him and his brain went blank as he lost the last thread of control over his body.

Careful not to wake Jess, Jackson withdrew his arm from around her waist and rolled onto his back. A comfortable exhaustion lapped at him. It would be so easy to curl back into Jess and sleep for hours. Too easy, which was a scary thought. They'd made love again. Slowly and sensually, and just as gratifying. She'd been generous in her lovemaking, and hungry for her own release. He hadn't experienced anything so straightforward and honest in a long time. And he'd enjoyed every moment.

But now he had to be thinking of getting home. Squinting at his watch, he tried to make out the time. Four twenty-four? The sun would soon be clawing its way up over the horizon. He slid out from under the sheet and groped around the floor for his clothes, which he took out to the bathroom to pull on.

He had to get away from here before there was a chance that anyone might see him leaving. He would not give anyone reason to gossip about Jess. It might be harmless but he knew how it could still hurt, ricocheting around the bay and getting more outrageous by the hour. According to Sasha, Jess wanted nothing more than to blend in around here, and to become a member of the community who everyone could rely on for help and empathy. She most definitely would not want to be the centre of idle chitchat at the corner store or in the pub. Jess wasn't as lucky as he and Sasha were, she didn't have her family to believe in her and stand by her.

Biting down on a sudden flare of anger, he dressed and headed to the kitchen to find pen and paper. He wouldn't leave without saying thank you. Or something. Anything but nothing. He did not want her waking up and thinking he'd done a dash while she'd slept because he hadn't had a good time or couldn't face her in the light of day.

Back in the bedroom he quietly crossed to place the note on her bedside table. Then he stood looking down at her in the glimmer of light from the bathroom opposite. Sleeping Jess appeared completely relaxed. No sass, no uncertainty. His heart lurched. And before he could think about it he bent down to kiss her warm cheek. His hand seemed to rise of its own volition and he had to snatch it back before he made the monumental error of cupping her face and leaning in for one of those brain-melting, hormone-firing kisses.

Another lurch in his chest. She was like a drug; slowing his thought processes, making him forget things he should never forget. So, he was already half under her influence. If he didn't leave immediately he might never go away. Which would cause all sorts of difficulties. He and Jessica were light years apart in what they wanted for their futures. Futures that could never blend comfortably. He didn't need the hassle of trying to make it work and failing, and neither did Jessica.

Walking away was hard, and for every step his heart made a loud thud against his ribs. But he had to—for Jess. Making sure the front door was locked behind him to keep her safe—which also meant he couldn't go back to her—he began the ten-kilometre walk back to his parents' house.

Hopefully, if anyone he or Jess knew happened by at this early hour they wouldn't put two and two together and come up with…four. Because there might be gossip about them spending the night together, but this was one story that would be based on truth.

Three hundred metres on and headlights swept over him. A car sped past, the horn tooting loud in the early morning. Again anger flared, sped along his veins. So much for being discreet. It just wasn't possible around here. Increasing his pace, he tried to outrun the temper threatening to overwhelm him. When would these surges of anger stop? It had been more than a month since the attack. He should have got past that terrifying night by now.

The nearly healed wound in his side pulled as Jackson swung his arms to loosen the knots in his neck and back. There was another reason for leaving before the sun came up. That bloody scar. If Jess saw it she'd have a stream of unwanted questions to fire his way. Somehow she hadn't noticed the rough ridge of puckered skin during the night. Amazing, considering he doubted there was a square millimetre of his body she hadn't touched at one time or another.

'So, Jackson,' he muttered, as he focused on the road and not tripping over some unseen obstacle in the semi light of dawn, 'where to from here, eh?'

His lips tightened as he grimaced.

'That's a tricky one. I don't want commitment, gossip

or questions about why I've got an ugly red scar on my body.' That about covered everything.

If only he'd worn running shoes he could be jogging now. Like they'd have been a good match for the wedding clobber he still wore. But who was around to notice? It was weird how quiet it was around here. No hordes of people bumping into him, no thousands of locals talking nonstop as they began their day. Very, very quiet. Peaceful. A complete contrast to Hong Kong.

'Don't get too comfortable. You're heading out of here before the end of April.' He spat the words. 'But I wouldn't mind a repeat of last night with Jess.' Just the mention of her name calmed him, slowed his angry thoughts. A smile began deep in his belly, sending tentacles of warmth to every corner of his body, curving his mouth upwards. 'Oh, yeah. I could do that all over again.'

But would he?

Even if it meant talking about things he preferred buried deep inside his psyche?

Right at this moment he had no damned idea.

CHAPTER THREE

KEEPING HER EYES closed, Jess reached across the bed for Jackson and came up cold. What? She scrambled up and looked around. She was alone.

'Jackson?' she called.

Nothing. No cheeky reply. No deep chuckle. Silence except for the house creaking as the sun warmed up the day.

'Great. Bloody wonderful, even. I hate it when the guy of the night before leaves without at least saying good bye.' Her stomach tightened. Jackson had enjoyed their lovemaking as much as she had. She'd swear to it. 'Maybe he didn't want the whole bay knowing we've been doing the deed.'

Was that good or bad? Did she want the whole of Golden Bay discussing her sex life? Nope. Definitely not. The muscles in her stomach released their death grip.

Did she want to do it again? With Jackson? Oh, yes. Her stomach tightened again. Absolutely wanted that. Which was a very good reason not to. Already she felt the need to see him pulling at her, wanted his arms around her, to hear his sexy chuckle. And that was after one night. Blimey. Was she falling for her best friend's brother? Even when she knew she shouldn't? That was a sure-fire way to fall out with Sasha, especially once

Jackson packed his bags and headed back to his job. But there was no helping those feelings of want and desire that seemed to sneak out of her skull when she wasn't looking.

Throwing the sheet aside, she leapt out of bed. He might've left but, darn, she felt good this morning. Despite the uncertainty of today and, in fact, every other day of the coming months with Jackson in the bay, she felt great. Just went to show what a healthy dose of sex could do for her.

'What's that?' A piece of paper lay on the floor by the bed. Picking it up, she read:

Hey, sleepyhead, thought I'd get away before the bay woke up. Thanks for a great night. See you at brunch. Hugs, Jackson.

Hugs, eh? That was good, wasn't it? Seemed he wasn't hiding from her if he'd mentioned the post-wedding brunch. What was the time? Eight-thirty. Yikes. She was supposed to be at the Wilsons' by nine-thirty and she had to pick up Nicholas. Her boy, the light of her life. She might've had a fantastic night but she missed him.

The piping-hot shower softened those aching muscles that had had a rare workout during the night. Singing loudly—and badly—she lathered shampoo through her hair while memories of last night with Jackson ran like a nonstop film through her mind. Hugging herself, she screeched out the words to a favourite song.

The phone was ringing as she towelled herself. Knowing she had no babies due at the moment, she wondered who'd be calling. Sasha would be too busy with Grady, it being the first day of married bliss and all that.

'Hello,' she sang.

'Is that Jessica Baxter? The midwife?' a strained male voice asked hesitantly.

Her stomach dropped. 'Yes, it is. Who's this?'

'You don't know me, but my wife's having a baby and I think something's wrong. It's too early. Can we come and see you? Like now?'

No. I'm busy. I'm going to have brunch with the most amazingly attractive, sexy-as-hell guy I've ever had the good luck to sleep with. Except, as of now, she wasn't. She swallowed the disappointment roiling in her stomach. 'Let's start at the beginning. Yes, I am Jessica. You are?'

'Sorry, I'm panicking a bit here. I'm Matthew Carter and my wife's Lily. We're up here for the weekend from Christchurch. Staying at Paton's Rock.' The more he talked the calmer he sounded. 'She seems a bit uncomfortable this morning.'

'How far along is your wife?' Why had they come away from home and their midwife when this Lily was due to give birth?

He hesitated, then, 'Nearly eight months. Everything's been good until this morning, otherwise we wouldn't have come away. But my cousin got married yesterday and we had to be here.'

'You were at Sasha and Grady's wedding?' She didn't remember seeing any obviously pregnant women, and as a midwife she usually noticed things like that.

'No, Greg and Deb Smith's.'

No one she knew. There were often multiple weddings in the bay in January. The golden beaches were a huge attraction for nuptials. 'Right. Tell me what's going on.'

'Lily's having pains in her stomach. Personally I think she ate too much rich food yesterday but she wants someone to check her out.'

'That sounds wise. They could be false labour pains.

Can you drive into Takaka and meet me at the maternity unit? It's behind the medical centre. I'll head there now.' She went on to give exact directions before hanging up.

Immediately picking the phone up again, she called the mother of Nicholas's friend and asked if it was all right for him to stay there a while longer. Then she phoned Sasha's mother.

'Virginia, I'm very sorry but I have to bail on brunch, or at least be very late. A pregnant woman from Christchurch is having problems.'

'That's fine, Jess. You can't predict when those babies will make their appearance.'

Yeah, but this wasn't one of hers. Then there was the fact it was coming early—if it was even coming at all. 'Can you tell Sasha and Grady I'm sorry? I really wanted to be there.' And can you let your son know too?

'Sure can. What about Jackson?'

Ahh. She swallowed. 'What about him?'

Virginia's laughter filled her ear. So that's where Jackson had got that deep chuckle. She'd never noticed Virginia's laugh before. 'Seems he had a bit of a walk home at daybreak. We shared a pot of tea when he got in. He doesn't realise how little I sleep these days. It gave him a bit of a shock when he crept in the back door just like he used to as a teenager.'

So much for Jackson trying to stop the town knowing about their night of fun. But his mother wouldn't be one for spreading that particular titbit of gossip. Or any other. She didn't do gossip. And…Jessica drew a breath…*she* didn't need to know what he'd got up to as a teen.

'Tell him thanks.' Oops. Wrong thing to blurt out to the man's mother.

'For what, Jess?' That laughter was back in Virginia's voice.

Too much information for Jackson's mother. 'For...' she cast around for something innocuous to say, came up blank.

Virginia's laughter grew louder. 'I'll tell him thanks. He can fill in the blanks. Good luck with the baby. Come round when you're done. We'd love to see you.'

I'm never going to the Wilson house again. My face will light up like a Christmas-tree candle the moment I step through their door. Apparently Virginia had a way of getting things out of a person without appearing to be trying.

Hauling on some knee-length shorts and a sleeveless shirt, she gave her hair a quick brush and tied it in a ponytail. There wasn't time to blow-dry it now and as she wasn't about to see Jackson it didn't really matter any more.

Pulling out of her driveway, she saw her neighbour, Mrs Harrop, waving at her from the front porch. They both lived on the outskirts of town in identical little houses built back in the 1950s. Mrs Harrop took care of the gardens for both of them while Jess made sure the other woman had proper meals every day by always cooking twice as much as she and Nicholas needed.

'Morning, Mrs Harrop. Everything all right with you today?'

'The sun came up, didn't it? How was the wedding? Who was that man I saw leaving your place in the early hours?' There was a twinkle in the seventy-year-old woman's eyes.

Damn. Usually her neighbour was half-blind in full daylight. 'Mrs Harrop...' Jess couldn't help herself. 'You won't mention anything to your friends, will you?'

'Get away with you, girl. My lips are zipped.'

Now, why did she have to mention zips? Jess's brain

replayed the memory of Jackson undoing the zip of her dress last night. Oh, and then of her hand on his fly, pulling that zip down. Turning the radio onto full blast, she sang some more cringeworthy words and banged the steering-wheel in an approximation of the song's beat, and drove to town.

Jess made it to the maternity unit fifteen minutes before the distressed couple arrived. She filled in the time making coffee and nipped next door to the store to buy a muffin for breakfast. Nothing like the big cook-up she could've been enjoying at the Wilson establishment. But way better for her waistline.

The man she supposed to be Matthew helped his wife into the clinic and stood hopping from foot to foot, looking lost and uncomfortable.

After the introductions, Jess helped Lily up onto the examination bed. 'This is where they used to tell the husbands to go and boil water.'

Matthew gave a reluctant smile. 'Thank goodness the world is far more modern these days. But I admit having something concrete to do would help me right now.'

'You could hold your wife's hand while I examine her.' Try being a comfort to her, rubbing her back. She's the one doing the hard work here.

'Speaking of water, Lily did pass a lot of fluid just before I rang you.'

'You're telling me her waters broke?' What was wrong with letting me know sooner?

Matthew looked sheepish. 'Lily wouldn't let me look and I wasn't sure.'

Jess wanted to bang her head against the wall and scream. These two really weren't dealing with this pregnancy very well. After an examination she told them,

'Baby's head's down, and its bottom is pointing up. You're definitely in labour.'

Lily said nothing, but her face turned white. 'Now? Here? We shouldn't have come.' The eyes she turned on her husband were filled with distress and something else Jess couldn't quite make out. Blame? Fear?

'Matthew told me you're nearly eight months along.' When Lily nodded slowly, Jessica groaned internally. She'd have preferred to be dealing with a full-term baby when she didn't know the patient. 'I need to talk to your midwife. Lily, have you timed how far apart your contractions are?'

'She wasn't sure they were contractions,' Matthew replied.

'So this is your first baby?' Jess asked.

'No, our second.' Matthew again.

So far Lily had hardly got a word in. Maybe that boiling water was a good idea after all. Jess pasted on a smile before saying, 'I really need to talk to Lily for a moment. Have you timed the pains?'

Lily nodded, her face colouring up. 'They're four minutes apart.'

'Okey-dokey, we've got a little lead-in time, then.' Possibly very little, if this baby was in a hurry, but there was no point in raising Lily's anxiety level any further. 'You can fill me in on details. Like who your midwife is and how I can get hold of her for a start.'

I so do not like flying blind. A perfectly normal pregnancy so far, according to Matthew, but that baby was coming early. Too early really. Jess punched the cellphone number Matthew read out from his phone.

'They're where?' the other midwife yelped when Jess explained the situation. 'I warned them not to leave town.

Lily has a history of early delivery. She's only thirty weeks. The last baby didn't survive.'

'Thirty weeks? You're sure? Sorry, of course you are. Damn it. Why would Matthew have said nearly eight months?' Jess would've sworn long and loud if it weren't the most unprofessional thing to do.

'To cover the fact he shouldn't have taken Lily away at all.' The other midwife didn't sound surprised.

'He's brought his wife to a place where there's no well-equipped hospital or any highly qualified obstetricians and paediatricians.' All because he'd wanted to go to a family wedding. The closest hospital by road was Nelson, a good two hours away. Now what? She had to call one of the local doctors. At least she knew where they all were. At the post-wedding brunch. She needed help fast. And probably a rescue helicopter. Those guys would have Lily in Nelson with every chance of saving her baby's life in a lot less time than any other form of transport.

Lily groaned her way through a contraction. It would only get worse very soon, Jess thought after another examination of Lily. 'Your baby has definitely decided on Golden Bay for its showdown.' But she'd do her damnedest to change that. 'Do you know if you're having a boy or a girl?'

'A girl,' Matthew answered.

A discreet knock at the door had her spinning around to see what her next crisis was. Another patient was not on her agenda.

Heat slammed into her tummy. 'Jackson?' Yes, please, thank you. 'Come in.' Perfect timing. 'What brought you here?'

'Mum's truck.' He grinned. 'When she told me why you'd phoned I thought I'd drop by and say hi.'

'I'm really glad you did.' Then Matthew glared at her and Jackson so she quickly made the introductions.

'Good. A doctor is exactly what we need,' the guy had the temerity to say straight to her face.

Lily would've had any number of those if only they'd stayed in Christchurch. 'Lily, Matthew, I need to talk to Dr Wilson. We'll be right back.'

She dragged Jackson out of the room before anyone had time to utter a word. Her hand held a bunch of his very expensive shirt, the likes of which wasn't usually seen around Takaka. In other circumstances, she'd have been pulling that gorgeous mouth down closer so she could kiss him hard and long. But today wasn't her lucky day. 'I know you don't start covering for Grady for a few more days so I can phone Mike or Roz, but I'd like some assistance here.' She quickly ran through all the details the midwife had given her. 'I think it would be best if the rescue helicopter is called. I do not want to risk that baby's life.'

'I'm with you.' Jackson caught her hand to his chest as she let go of his shirt. 'The baby will need all the support it can get right from the moment it appears.'

'She. It's a girl.' Jess spread her fingers across the chest that only hours ago she'd been kissing. 'You need to make the call. I'm not authorised to except in exceptional circumstances.' Which this could arguably be.

'No problem. I'll examine Lily first and then I'll know what I'm talking about when I phone the rescue service. Can you get me the number? And the midwife's? I'd like to talk to her, too.' His green gaze was steady. 'I'm not undermining you, Jess. I prefer first-hand information, that's all. Especially since it's been a while since I delivered a baby.'

The relief that he was sharing the burden swamped

her, although she knew it shouldn't. She had experience in difficult deliveries, though always in places where back-up was on hand. 'Not a problem, I assure you.' She turned to head for her patient. 'Come on, we'll talk to those two again. Together.'

Jackson still held her hand, tugged her back against him. 'I had a great time.' His lips brushed hers. 'Thank you.'

You and me both. But she couldn't tell him because of the sudden blockage in her throat and the pounding in her ears. So she blinked and smiled and then made her way into see Lily.

Jackson made the phone calls and returned to check on baby Carter's progress. He was angry.

Breathe deep, in one two, out one two.

This mother and baby should not be here, jeopardising their chances of a good outcome. His hands fisted.

In one two. Out one two.

Sure, everything could work out perfectly, but at thirty weeks the baby would still need an incubator and special care. The father was a moron. Especially considering the fact their last baby had died. How did Jess remain so calm? Maybe she'd had time to settle down and get on with what mattered most, appearing confident in the current situation and ignoring the if-only's. 'Lily, you're going to Nelson Hospital to have this baby. It's too early for us to be bringing her into the world here.' His tone was too harsh.

In one two. Out one two.

'I'm not driving Lily over that awful hill in her condition. It was uncomfortable enough for her on Friday and she wasn't in labour then.' Matthew stared at Jackson as though it was his fault they were dealing with this here and now.

Jackson ground his teeth and fought for control. Losing his temper would do absolutely nothing to help. Finally, on a very deep, indrawn breath, he managed to explain without showing his anger. 'The rescue helicopter will be here in approximately one hour. Jessica, where do they land?'

'In the paddock out the back of the medical centre. I'll go and see if there are any sheep that need shifting. Matthew, you can give me a hand.' Jess winked at Jackson before she led the startled man out the door.

'Go, Jess.' Jackson grinned to himself, his anger easing off quicker than usual. Starting an examination of Lily, he talked to her all the while, explaining what was happening. And calmed down further. These sudden anger spurts were disturbing. He was usually known for his cool, calm manner in any crisis and he'd hoped taking time away from his job would fix the problem. It seemed he was wrong or maybe just impatient.

'Will my baby be all right?' Lily asked through an onset of tears.

He would not promise anything. 'We'll do everything we can towards that outcome.'

The tears flowed harder. 'I didn't want to come to the wedding but Matthew insisted. He can be very determined.'

Try selfish and stubborn. 'We can't change the fact that you're in Golden Bay at the moment so let's concentrate on keeping baby safe.'

'Grr. Ahhh.' Lily's face screwed up with pain as another contraction tore through her.

Jackson reached for a flailing hand, held it tightly. The contractions were coming faster. All he could do was prepare for the birth and hope like hell the emergency crew would get here first. How fast could they spin those rotors? Where was Jess? She'd be more at ease with the situation than him. It's what she did, bringing babies into the world. Admittedly not usually this early or with this much danger of things going horribly wrong, but she was still more used to the birthing process.

'Hey, how are we doing?' A sweet voice answered his silent pleas. Jess had returned, dissolving the last of the tension gripping him.

Stepping away from the bed and closer to this delightful woman who seemed to have a way about her that quickly relaxed him, he murmured, 'Remind me to buy you another bottle of champagne when this is over.'

The fudge-coloured eyes that turned to him were twinkling. Her citrus tang wafted in the air when she leaned close to whisper, 'I might need some of that brunch first. My energy levels need rebuilding.'

Jess would drive him crazy with need if he wasn't careful. And did that matter? Of course it did. Didn't it? He'd hate to hurt her in any way. 'You'll have to wait. How was that paddock? Any sheep?'

'Nope, all clear. The windsock is hardly moving so the landing should be straightforward. How's Lily doing?'

'Starting to panic. And who can blame her?'

Jess crossed to the woman. 'We're all set for that helicopter, Lily. Ever been in one before?'

'N-no. I—I don't like flying.'

Jackson groaned quietly. This day was going from bad to worse for the woman. 'They're quite different to being in a plane. Perfectly safe. The pilot will probably go around the coastline instead of over the hill so you won't be too far above ground level.'

Jess added, 'This is definitely the best way to keep

your baby safe. Now, with the next contraction I want you to stand. You might find it easier to deal with the pain.'

Lily's smile was strained as she clambered off the bed. 'Thank you. I know you're trying your best. I'll be okay.' Then all talk stopped as she went through another contraction.

This time Matthew held her as she draped herself over him and hung on. 'You're doing great, Lily.'

Finally, just when Jackson thought they'd be delivering Baby Carter in the medical centre the steady thwup-thwup of the helicopter approaching reached them inside the hot and stuffy room. 'Here we go. Your ride has arrived, Lily,' he said needlessly.

Everyone had heard the aircraft and Matthew had gone to watch the landing. Jackson followed him out and once the rotors had stopped spinning he strode across to meet the paramedic and paediatrician as they disembarked and began unloading equipment.

'Glad to see that incubator.' He nodded towards the interior of the craft. 'You might be needing it.'

'Baby's that close?' the man who'd introduced himself as Patrick asked. His arm badge read 'Advanced Paramedic'.

'The mother has the urge to push. But I'm hoping she can hold off for a bit longer.'

'Let's take a look before we decide how to run with it. I don't fancy a birth in mid-air.'

In the end, Baby Carter made their minds up for them. She arrived in a hurry, sliding out into the bright light of the world, a tiny baby that barely filled Jackson's hand. Handing her carefully to Jess, he concentrated on repairing a tear that Lily had received during the birth.

Matthew stood to one side, stunned at the unfolding events. 'Is Lily okay? What about my daughter? Is she going to make it? At least she cried. That's got to be good, doesn't it?'

The last baby didn't cry? Jackson looked up and locked gazes with Matthew. 'The baby's breathing normally, and Lily's going to be fine. Have you decided on a name for your daughter?'

'Yes, but we were afraid to mention it until we knew if she'd be all right.' Matthew's eyes shifted to the right, where his daughter was being attached to monitors inside the incubator. 'Alice Rose,' he whispered, and brushed the back of his hand over his face.

'Alice Rose Carter.' Jess spared the man a sympathetic glance. 'I like it. Pretty. And so is she. Come over here and see for yourself.'

The paediatrician continued adjusting equipment as he explained, 'Alice Rose is very small, as to be expected. At thirty weeks her lungs aren't fully developed so this machine will help her breathe until she grows some. But…' the man looked directly at Matthew '…everything so far shows she's looking to be in good shape despite her early arrival. I'm not saying you're out of trouble yet. There are a lot of things to watch out for, but one step at a time, eh?'

Matthew blinked, swiped at his face again and stepped closer to his daughter. 'Hello, Alice. I'm your daddy.' Then he sniffed hard.

Jess handed the guy a box of tissues. 'Hey, Daddy, blow your nose away from your baby.' She said it in such a soft tone that Jackson knew she'd forgiven the guy for being rather highhanded earlier. 'You're going to have to learn to be very careful around Alice Rose for a long time to come.'

Jackson helped Lily into a sitting position. 'I'm so sorry you can't hold your daughter yet.' That had to be devastating for any new mother. During many long phone calls last year Sasha had often told him that she could barely wait for Melanie to be placed in her arms and to be able to give her that very first kiss. Lily and Matthew weren't going to have that for a while.

'I'm grateful she's doing all right so far. Not like last time. We knew straight away little Molly wouldn't make it.' Lily's bottom lip trembled. 'No. I'm lying. I want to hold her so much it hurts. By the time I do she won't be a newborn.' The tears flowed, pouring down her cheeks to soak into the hospital gown that she still wore.

'You're going to need to head across to Nelson as soon as possible,' Jackson told her, shifting the subject to more practical matters. 'There's a shower next door, if you want to clean up first.'

'Thank you. It all seems surreal. I've just been through childbirth and there's no baby in my arms to show for it.' Tears sparkled out of her tired eyes as she gathered up her clothes and headed towards the bathroom.

His heart squeezed. For this couple who'd blown into their lives that morning with a monumental problem? Or could there be more to his emotional reaction? Since the attack he'd never quite known where his emotions were taking him, they were so out of whack. Coming home had added to his unrest. Having spent so many years being thankful that he'd escaped Golden Bay, it was difficult to understand why regrets were now filtering through his long-held beliefs.

He'd never really given much thought to having a family of his own. It wasn't that he didn't want one. It was just a thought that had been on the back burner while he established his career and got over his distrust of women enough to get to really know them. Then his career had grown into a two-headed monster, leaving him little time to develop anything remotely like a relationship. The women who'd passed through his life hadn't changed that opinion. Probably because he'd chosen women who wouldn't want to wreck their careers or their figures by having children. He'd chosen women who wouldn't lie to him or about him.

But honestly? He wasn't against a relationship where he settled down with someone special. The problem was, he couldn't see it working in the centre of Hong Kong surrounded by high-rises and very little green space. As that city was where his life came together, where he was the man he'd strived so hard to become, he could see that there'd be no children in his life for a long while.

He looked around and found Jess regarding him from under lowered eyelids. Could she read him? Did she know that if he ever changed his mind she might be the one woman he'd be interested in? Get a grip, Jackson. Until last night he wouldn't even have had these thoughts. One very exciting and enjoyable night in the arms of Jessica Baxter and he was getting some very weird ideas.

Because, love or hate Golden Bay, there was a lot to be said for the outdoors lifestyle and bringing up kids in this district. The district where his career would fizzle out with the lack of hospitals and emergency centres.

CHAPTER FOUR

THE HELICOPTER LIFTED off the paddock, the wind it created whipping at Jess's clothes, moulding her shirt against her breasts. 'Right, I'd better go and pick up Nicholas. I promised he would get to see Sasha and Grady before they left on their honeymoon.' Jess glanced at her watch. 'Brunch is probably well and truly wrapped up by now.'

Jackson's gaze was on her breasts. 'What did you say?' he almost shouted.

She grinned. Deafened by the aircraft or distracted by her boobs? 'I need to collect Nicholas. And hopefully catch Sasha and Grady before they leave.'

Jackson finally lifted his head enough to meet her gaze. 'Okay.' He tossed his keys up and down in his left hand. 'I don't think they were heading off until about one. Their flight leaves Nelson at four and they're staying overnight in Auckland.'

'Two weeks in Fiji sounds sublime.' Jess sighed wistfully and headed inside.

'Not just Fiji, but Tokariki Island. Tiny place, catering for only a few couples at a time. Heaven.' Jackson grinned at her as he strode alongside, sending those butterflies in her stomach on another of their merry dances.

'You are so mean. I'd love to go to the Islands.' With a hot man. Not that it was ever going to happen. She was a mother with a four-year-old who needed her more than anyone. 'Let's get out of here before the bell rings and we're stuck fixing cuts and scrapes for the rest of the day.' Leading by example, she turned off the lights and headed for the outside door.

'Can I come with you to pick up your son?'

Jess stopped her mad dash for freedom and spun round to come chest to chest with Jackson. He'd startled her with his simple request, and judging by the look of surprise in his eyes he'd startled himself as well. 'Did I hear right? You want to share a tiny car with a loud, boisterous little boy who talks nonstop, never letting anyone else get a word in?'

She waited for him to back off fast. But instead he nodded. 'Guess I do. Is Nicholas really that noisy?'

Laughter rolled up her throat. 'Oh, boy. You have no idea.' This would test their burgeoning friendship. Her son was no angel. In fact, she had to admit he was getting very much out of control and she didn't know what to do about it. Loving him to bits meant saying no which didn't come easily for her.

But one day soon she was going to have to grow a backbone when it came to Nicholas or they were in for a very rocky ride as he grew up. It was just that she needed to lavish him with love, show him how much he mattered to her. She would not become her parents, throwing money at every situation when more often than not a hug would have sufficed. No. Nicholas would always know how much she cared about him. Always.

A big, warm and strong hand cupped her chin, tilted her head back so that she stared into Jackson's green gaze. 'Jess? Where have you gone? Something up?'

With an abrupt shake of her head she stepped away from that hand and those all-seeing eyes. It would be too easy to lean into him, burden him with her problems. That would certainly put the kibosh on getting to know him better. He'd suddenly have so much to do she'd not even see his delectable butt departing for all the dust he'd raise on the way out. She mightn't be sophisticated but she knew the rules. She'd invented some of them.

Keep it simple.

Do not get too close.

Don't ask him for more than fun. And great sex.

Her skin sizzled. What they'd shared last night had gone beyond fun, beyond description. She grimaced. What rule had she broken there?

'Jessica, you're going weird on me.' Jackson was right beside her as she punched in the security code for the alarm system.

Pulling the door shut and checking it was locked, she dug deep for a nonchalant answer and came up with, 'Not weird, just pulling on my mother-in-charge persona.'

'You're two different people?' His eyes widened, making him look surprised and funny at the same time.

She couldn't keep serious around him. Bending forward at the waist, one hand on her butt like a tail and the other creating a beak over her mouth, she headed towards her car. 'Quack, quack, quack.'

'Hang on, who are you? Where's Jess gone? Bring her back. I'm not getting in a vehicle with a duck.'

'Quack, quack.'

Jackson chuckled. 'Is this how you bring up your son? The poor little blighter. He'll be scarred for life. I need to save him.'

Jess felt his arms circle her and swing her off the ground to be held against that chest she'd so enjoyed running her fingers up and down during the night. She slid her hands behind his neck and grinned into his face. 'You're not going to kiss a duck?'

He groaned. 'I must be as crazy as you.' Then his mouth covered hers and she forgot everything except his kiss.

Heat spiralled out of control inside her. Her skin lifted in excited goose-bumps. Between her legs a steady throb of need tapped away at her sanity. Sparks flew. Whoever had invented electricity obviously hadn't had great sex.

Without taking that gorgeous, sexy mouth away from hers, Jackson set her on her feet and tugged her hard against him. She could feel his reaction to her against her abdomen. She clung to him. To stop holding him would mean ending up in an ungainly heap on the ground.

His lips lifted enough for him to demand, 'What's that code you just punched in?'

'Why?'

'We need a bed. Or privacy at least.'

He was right. They couldn't stay in the very public car park, demonstrating their awakening friendship. Not when he'd made sure no one had seen him leaving her place early that morning. She glanced down at Jackson's well-awake evidence of their needs and grinned. 'Three-two-four-eight-one.'

'I'm expected to remember that in the midst of a wave of desire swamping my brain?'

Thank goodness he returned his mouth to hers the moment he'd got that question out. She couldn't stand it when he withdrew from kissing her. Could this man kiss or what?

Cheep-cheep. Cheep-cheep.

'What the—?' Jackson's eyes were dazed as he looked around.

Reality kicked into Jess. 'My phone.' She tugged the

offending item from her pocket and glared at the screen. Then softened. 'It's probably Nicholas, using Andrea's phone.' As she pressed the talk button she gave Jackson an apologetic shrug. 'This is another side of being a mother. Always on call.' Then, 'Hello, is that my boy?'

'Mummy, where are you? I want to see Grady now.' He'd taken to Grady very quickly. Perhaps it was a sign he needed a male figure in his life?

'I'm on my way to get you.' She turned from the disappointment in Jackson's eyes. He might as well get used to the reality of her life right from the start. Presuming he wanted to see more of her, and that bulge in his jeans suggested he did.

'How long will you be, Mummy? I want to show you the fish the seagulls stole.'

'Nicholas, you know I can't talk to you while I'm driving so you'll have to wait until I get there to tell me about the seagulls. Okay?'

'Why won't the policemen let you drive and talk to me? It's not fair.'

Jess grinned. 'It's the law, sweetheart.' Knowing Nicholas could talk for ever, she cut him off. 'See you soon.'

Jackson's hands were stuffed into the pockets of his designer jeans as he leaned against the vehicle he'd borrowed from his mother. 'Want me to drive?'

'You still want to come with me?' Now, that surprised her. As far as she knew, Jackson wasn't used to little kids and this particular one had interrupted something fairly intense. 'Are you going to growl at him for his timing?'

'No.' He flicked a cheeky smile her way. 'The day will come when someone interrupts him in his hour of need.'

She groaned and slapped her forehead. 'I do not want to think about that. He's four, not thirty-four.'

'Thirty-four?'

'That's when I'll think about letting him out on his own to see girls.'

'Good luck with that one.' He crossed to the driver's side of her car and held his hand up for the keys. 'Let's go.'

'Um, my car. I drive.'

He just grinned at her. Really grinned, so that her tummy flip flopped and her head spun. So much that driving could be dangerous.

'Go on, then.' She tossed the keys over the top of her car. 'Men.'

'Glad you noticed.'

How could she not? His masculinity was apparent in those muscles that filled his jeans perfectly, in his long-legged stride, in the jut of his chin, in that deep, sexy chuckle that got her hormones in a twitter every time. She climbed into the passenger seat and closed the door with a firm click. Then something occurred to her. 'We're going to Pohara Beach. Shouldn't we take both vehicles, save a trip back into town later?'

'Nah. I'll go for a run when it cools down, pick up the truck then. Mum won't be needing it today.'

'Running? As in pounding the pavement and building up a sweat?' She shuddered. 'You obviously need a life.' But it did explain those superb thigh muscles. And his stamina.

Jackson just laughed. 'You're not into jogging, then? Knitting and crochet more your style?'

Thinking about the cute little jerseys she'd made for Nicholas last winter, she smiled and kept quiet. *If only you knew, Jackson.*

Then he threw another curve ball as they headed towards the beach. 'Who held you while you had Nicholas? Who smoothed your back and said you were doing fine?'

The man wasn't afraid of the big questions. 'No one ever asked me that before.' Not even Mum and Dad. Especially not Mum and Dad.

'Tell me to shut up if you want.'

That was the funny thing. She didn't want to. Jackson touched something in her that negated all her usual reticence when it came to talking about personal things. 'Two nurses I was friendly with took it in turns to hold my hand and talk me through the pain.' She'd trained with Phillip and Rochelle, and when they'd got married she'd been there to celebrate with them. They'd been quick to put their hands up when she'd announced she was having a baby, offering to help in any way they could. It had been more than three years since they'd left to work in Australia, and she still missed them.

'That must've been hard.'

Because Nicholas's dad wasn't there? No, by then she'd known she'd had a lucky escape. 'Not so bad. It was worse afterwards when I wanted to share Nicholas's progress, to talk about him and know I was on the right track with how I brought him up. That's when single mothers have it tough. That's what I've been told, and going by my own experience I have to agree.' It was also probably why Nicholas got away with far more than he should. There was no one to share the discipline, to play good cop, bad cop with.

'So how do you cope with the day-to-day stuff of being a solo mum?'

'Heard of the headless chook? That's me.'

'When you're not being a duck, you mean?'

She giggled. 'That too. I don't think about how I manage, I just do. I wouldn't want to go back to before I had Nicholas. Being a mother is wonderful. Though there are days when I go to visit Sasha or your mum for a bit of adult conversation and to help calm the worry that I'm getting it all wrong.'

'Even two parents bringing up a child together have those worries.'

'Guess it will never stop.'

Jackson turned onto the road running beside Pohara Beach. 'I was watching Lily and Matthew earlier. They were desperate to hold their baby and it hurt them not to be able to.'

Again she thought she could read him. 'Believe me, if you want to be a part of your child's life then you're not going to miss that first cuddle for anything. Sad to say, but my boy's father truly didn't care. He came to town for three months, had a lot of fun, and left waving a hand over his shoulder when I told him I was pregnant. He didn't even say goodbye.'

It was silent in the car for a minute then she pointed to a sprawling modern home on the waterfront. 'There.'

Jackson pulled up on the drive, switched the engine off and turned to her. 'He wasn't interested in his child?'

'There was a wife in Alaska.' It had hurt so much at the time. She'd been an idiot to fall for him.

'The jerk.' Jackson lifted her hand and rubbed his thumb across the back of it, sending shivers of need racing through her blood. Again.

'It's Nicholas who misses out. He'd love a dad to do all those male things with. Apparently I'm no good at football.' She pushed out of the car. All the better to breathe. Despite the conversation they were having, sitting beside Jackson in her minuscule car did nothing to quieten her rampaging hormones.

'Mummy, here I am.' Nicholas's sweet voice interrupted her internal monologue and reminded her who was important in her life. Here was the only person she should be thinking about.

'Hey, sweetheart, have you had a good time?' She reached out to haul him in for a hug but he'd stumbled to a stop and banged his hands on his hips.

His head flipped back at Jackson. 'What's your name?' he demanded.

Jackson stood on the other side of the car, studying her boy in that searching way of his. 'I'm Jackson Wilson. You saw me at the wedding.' He came round and put his hand out to be shaken.

But Nicholas hadn't finished. 'Why did you drive my mummy's car?'

The corner of Jackson's mouth lifted but he kept his amusement under control. 'I like driving and haven't been doing very much lately.'

'Mummy likes driving, too.' Nicholas stared at the proffered hand. 'Are you a friend of ours?'

'Yes, I am. That's why I'm waiting to shake your hand. Want to put yours in mine, sport?'

Jess could barely contain her laughter as she watched her son strut across and bang his tiny hand into Jackson's much larger one. They both shook.

'See, Mummy. That's how it's done.'

'So it is.' What she did see was that Nicholas really did need some male influence in his life. He picked up on anything Grady said, and now, if she wasn't mistaken, he was factoring Jackson into his thinking.

A chill ran through her veins. Not good. Jackson would soon be going away again, and if Nicholas got too fond of him, they were in for tears. Some of those might be hers, too. Already she felt comfortable around him in a way she rarely felt with men. There were a lot of hidden depths to Jackson, but she liked the way he took the proper time with her son. Amongst other things. Then her face heated as she recalled how there'd been no time spared last night when they'd first fallen into bed.

'Do I get my hug now, Nicholas?'

Dropping the strut, her boy ran at her, barrelling into her legs. 'I missed you, Mummy. Did you miss me?'

Swinging him up in her arms, she grinned and kissed his cheek. 'Big time.'

'Hi, Jess,' Andrea called from the porch of the house. 'How was the wedding?'

Andrea's question might have been directed to Jessica but her gaze was fixed on Jackson. He seemed to have that effect on most women. Including her. Even now, when there was no alcohol fizzing around her system, she definitely had the hots for him. She knew that if they were alone with time to spare she'd be requesting a repeat performance of last night's lovemaking.

But she wasn't alone with him. Her son was waiting to go and see Grady, and Andrea was waiting for a reply to her question. 'Sasha looked stunning, and Grady scrubbed up all right, too. They're leaving on their honeymoon shortly so I'd better get Nicholas around there to say goodbye. Thank you so much for having him to stay. I hope he wasn't any trouble.' He could be. She knew that. He hated being told what to do and could throw a paddy that matched the severity of a tornado. It was something she needed to work on.

He wriggled to be set down as Andrea waved a hand in his direction. 'You were very well behaved, weren't you, Nicholas? I wish Bobby could be half as good.'

Huh? Did Nicholas only play up for her? 'Thank goodness for that.' Jess checked he'd put his seat belt on properly before walking around to get back in the car.

Jackson started backing out the driveway. 'What did you get up to with your friend, Nicholas?'

'We played soccer, and Bobby's dad took us in his truck to get a boat. I wanted to go fishing but we weren't allowed because no adults wanted to go with us.' On and on he went, detailing every single thing he'd done since she'd dropped him off after the wedding service and before the reception.

Warmth stole through her, lifting her lips into a smile. 'That's my boy,' she whispered. Though thankfully they were pulling up outside Virginia and Ian's within minutes. Jess didn't want Jackson bored to sleep while driving. But he was the one to unclip Nicholas's belt and help him down. 'There you go, sport. Let's see if there's any of that brunch left for us to enjoy.'

'What's brunch?'

'Breakfast and lunch all mixed together,' Jess told him as she straightened his shirt.

'Why do you mix them?'

'So you only have one meal.' She rubbed his curls and got a glare for her trouble.

'That's a dumb idea.' Nicholas, as usual, got in the last word.

There were still a lot of people milling around, obviously in no hurry to leave. Jess hoped Virginia was coping. Yesterday had been tiring enough for someone with her disease. 'I'm going to see if I can do anything to help,' she told Jackson.

'I'll go and find Dad,' he told her.

'Hey, there you two are.' Grady strode across the lawn towards them.

The way he said it suggested she and Jackson were a couple. That would surely send Jackson off to hide amongst the guests.

'Howdy, Grady. How's married life treating you so far?' she asked.

'No complaints,' he answered, before swinging Nicholas up above his head and holding the giggling, writhing body of her son aloft. 'Hey, Nicholas, how are you doing, boyo? Did you have fun at Bobby's house?'

'Yes, yes,' Nicholas shrieked. 'Make me fly, Grady.'

'Please,' Jess said automatically.

Too late. Grady swooped his armful earthward and up again. How his back took the strain she had no idea. 'Where's Sasha?'

'Inside with Virginia, getting some more food. Man, these people can eat.' Swoop, and Nicholas was flying towards the ground again.

'You okay with Nicholas while I go see what I can do to help?' she asked Grady.

'She thinks I can't look after you, Nicholas. Women, eh?'

'What do you mean, women?' Nicholas's little face screwed up in question.

Jackson laughed. 'Get yourself out of that in one piece, Grady.'

'Better that he knows all he can as soon as possible.' Grady grinned. 'Leave the lad with us, Jess. We'll teach him all our bad habits.'

'That's what I'm afraid of.' She tipped her head to one side. 'You are grinning a lot this morning, Mr O'Neil. I'd better go see what Mrs O'Neil has been up to.' Jess headed to the house, ignoring the ribald comments coming from the two men she'd just left.

Inside she found Sasha and Virginia busy plating up leftover dessert from the wedding dinner. One look at Sasha told her everything. 'Oh, yuk. You look as happy as Grady. Must be something in the water out here.'

Sasha grinned and rushed to hug her. 'Morning. You're not looking too unhappy yourself.'

Uh-oh. Jess looked over at Virginia who suddenly seemed very busy placing slices of fruit on a pavlova. 'Of course I do. I've just delivered a baby. Although she was ten weeks early.'

'Is that why the helicopter went over earlier?' Virginia finally lifted her head. Dark shadows stained her cheeks, and her smile was a little loose.

'Yep. Now, Virginia, I'd love nothing better than a good old chinwag with Sasha before she leaves on her honeymoon. Want to let me finish that while I talk? Jackson's outside somewhere.'

Jess held her breath. She knew better than to out and out insist that Sasha's mum should take a rest.

'Good idea. I've been waiting to have a chat with that boy of mine.' She had the audacity to wink at Jess.

'I think he's with Grady, though he said he wanted to find Ian.'

Virginia hadn't even got to the door when Sasha rounded on Jess, grabbing her arms. 'What's this about my brother staying the night at your place?'

Didn't Sasha approve? She should have known it wasn't wise to get too close to her friend's brother. Hell, none of last night had been wise, but it had been a lot of fun. Though if it would come between her and Sasha then she'd learn to get over Jackson fast. Which wasn't a bad idea. She didn't want a serious relationship. 'Your mother's been talking?'

'Her words were, "Maybe there's enough of an attraction here to keep Jackson from returning to Hong Kong."' Sasha locked her eyes on Jess's, looking right inside her. 'It's okay, you know. In fact, I wholeheartedly approve.'

The air in Jess's lungs whooshed across her lips. 'I'm

glad it isn't going to be an issue between us. But you and your mother are getting ahead of the game. One night doesn't automatically lead to a wedding.'

'Got to start somewhere.' Sasha grinned again.

These lovesick grins were getting tiresome. But, then, hadn't she been smiling and laughing more than normal this morning? 'Great sex does the trick every time.'

'Excuse me?' Sasha's eyebrows rose and her brow wrinkled.

'You and Grady, going around like those clowns at the show with big grins that won't close.'

'Oh. Like the one on your face right now? Bet there's one on my brother's mug, too.'

Jess couldn't help it. She burst out laughing, and grabbed Sasha into another hug. 'Guess we should get these pavlovas done.'

'You always change the subject when it gets too hot for you.' Sasha resumed hulling the bowl of strawberries on the bench beside her. 'By the way, thank you for that painting you gave us. It's fabulous. How does the artist do such intricate work? Looking at that gull on the post with the sea in the background makes me feel the sun on my face and the salt air in my nostrils.'

'He's very good, no doubt about it.'

'Yeah, well, we love it and thank you so much. Of course, I could say you shouldn't have spent that kind of money but then I'd have to give the painting back and I'm not parting with it.'

'Damn. My cunning plan failed.'

They talked about the wedding as they worked, reminding each other of everything that had happened from the moment they'd started getting ready early yesterday morning.

Loud masculine laughter reached them through the

open kitchen windows and Jess stopped to stare out at Jackson as he stood talking with Grady and Ian. Those butt-hugging jeans and a T-shirt that outlined his well-defined muscles made her mouth water. Her heart bumped harder and louder than normal, and those pesky butter-flies in her tummy started their dance again. 'Sasha, what does love feel like?' she whispered.

Sasha came to stand beside her and looked in the same direction. Slipping her arm through Jess's, she answered softly, 'It feels like every day is summer, like the air is clearer, and at night the stars are brighter. Love feels as though nothing can go wrong. As though everything is bigger. It makes you laugh and smile more.'

Jess bit down hard on her lip. *I've fallen in love. Over-night. Or did it happen the moment I saw Jackson stand-ing beside Grady as they waited for us to arrive and the wedding ceremony to start? Does it even matter? It's happened. And it's not going anywhere.*

Sasha nudged her gently. 'The sky's very blue today, isn't it? Sparkling with sunlight.'

'Yes,' she whispered. *What the heck do I do now?*

'The colour of love, I reckon.'

CHAPTER FIVE

'WHO'S LOOKING AFTER Nicholas while you're working all these extra hours?' Jackson asked Jessica, as she folded the towels just back from the laundry and stacked them in the storeroom. It was Wednesday and he'd missed her every minute since the weekend. At least working here at the medical centre he got to see her occasionally but most of the time they were both too busy for more than quick snatches of conversation.

'He's at day care until Andrea picks him up after she collects her little boy from school. Bobby started school on Monday and Nicholas is so jealous. June can't come quickly enough for him.'

'I bet. It must be hard to leave him while you work.' She doted on her boy.

'It is. His little face turns all sad, which hurts to see. But it only happens a couple of days a week unless I'm covering for someone here.' Her face was turning sad now.

'You wouldn't think of not working at all?' What was her financial situation?

'Thanks to my parents…' she winced '…I could afford to stay at home, but not having a partner I need some adult contact. The brain needs some exercise, too.'

'I can understand that. It won't hurt Nicholas to be

mixing with other kids his age either.' Do not wrap her up in a hug. Not here at work. 'Do you like doing Sasha's job as well as your own?' From what he'd seen so far, she coped remarkably well. Nothing seemed too much for her. It made him wonder if people took advantage of that.

Jessica shrugged. 'Two weeks is nothing. And I get to keep my other nursing skills up to date.'

'Do you often do the nursing job?'

'First and foremost I'm the midwife, but if either nurse wants time off I cover for her. I like the variety and there are times when I've got no babies due and need to be busy.' The face she lifted to him was beautiful. Those big brown eyes were shining and her mouth had been curved in a perpetual smile all day.

'That chicken dish you dropped at home yesterday was tasty. When did you find the time to make it?' He and Dad had come in from the orchard late to find that Jess had dropped by with the meal. 'Mum was grateful, though, be warned, she's not likely to tell you.'

'I know. Not a problem. The wedding took its toll on her.'

'Which is why I haven't had time to call round to see you since Sunday.' Not for lack of trying. 'Dad's had a lot to do, clearing away everything and getting on with the orchard needs.' He'd ached to visit Jess but knew his priorities lay with his parents for a few days at least. His guilt at not having been here for so long could only be kept at bay by working his butt off, doing chores for them. Leaving in April was not going to be easy. 'My tractor skills have been in demand.'

'I understand.' The hand she laid on his arm was warm, but the sensations zipping through his blood were red hot. 'Virginia's worked nonstop on wedding plans since the day Sasha proposed to Grady. She had to crash some time.'

Jackson grinned. 'Sasha proposed to Grady? Are you sure?'

Nodding, Jess told him, 'Absolutely. She did it minutes after Melanie was born.'

'That's so Sasha. I'd have thought Grady would've been chomping at the bit to ask her to marry him. He's besotted.'

'Isn't he? Sasha had been keeping him at a distance. Afraid he might leave her again, I guess.'

Jackson stepped back, away from the citrus scent, away from that body that he so craved. Otherwise he was going to haul Jess into his arms and kiss her senseless. Something he wanted to do every time he saw her. Something he very definitely couldn't do while at work in the medical centre. But they could catch up out of the work zone. 'I've been checking the tides and it's looking good for a spot of surfcasting. How about we take Nicholas down to the beach when we're done here and he can try some fishing?'

Her eyes were definitely fudge-coloured right now. 'You'd do that? I'd love it, and you'll be Nicholas's hero for ever.' Then the light gleaming out at him dimmed. 'Maybe that's not so wise.'

Jackson stepped back close, laid his hands on her shoulders. 'I promise to be careful with him. And Grady will be back to replace me in my male role model position.' He suddenly didn't like that idea. Not one little bit. For a brief moment he wished he could be the man who showed Nicholas the ways of the world. But he wasn't being realistic at all. It was not possible to be there for Nicholas for more than a few weeks. So having Grady in the background was good. He had to believe that, or go crazy, worrying about the little guy.

Under his hands her shoulders lifted, dropped. 'You're right. But just so as you know, I don't want Nicholas getting high expectations of your involvement with him. Not when you're not staying around.'

At least she hadn't said anything about his involvement with her. While he hadn't worked out where their relationship was headed, he didn't want the gate closing before they'd spent more time together. 'I understand, Jess.'

'Do you?' She locked her gaze on him, like she was searching for something. 'I worry because I know what it's like to have expectations of adults and never have them met.'

'Your parents?' He held his breath, waiting for her to tell him to go to hell. To say it was none of his business.

But after a moment she nodded. 'Yeah. I'm sure they loved me. But they never needed me. I was a nuisance when all they needed was each other and their busy life outdoors, studying native flora and fauna, and how to protect it for generations to come. They tried. I'll give them that. I always had more money than even I could spend. Occasionally they took me on trips to places in the world most people aren't even aware of. All far away from civilisation, from the fun things a kid likes to do. I guess growing up I never wanted for anything. Except hugs, and sharing girl talk with my mother, and being able to brings friends home for sleepovers.'

When she started spilling her heart she didn't stop easily. The pain in her words cut him deep. No one should ever feel that they came second best with their parents. No one. To hell with being at the medical centre. He wrapped his arms around her, held her tight, and dropped kisses on the top of her head. 'You already give Nicholas far more than that.'

'I hope so,' she murmured against him, her warm breath heating his skin. 'It's a work in progress.'

'You think you don't know how to love? From what I've seen, you're spot on.' She exuded love—to Nicholas, to Sasha, his parents, her patients. Did she have any left over for him? Because he really wanted some. Correction, he wanted lots. And what would he give her in return? Love? Full, hands-on love? Or the chilly, remote kind, like her parents'? From afar, in a city that was not conducive to raising a small boy with an apparent penchant for the outdoors.

His hands dropped away and he took that backwards step again. It was too soon to know. Did he want to know? He knew he didn't want to hurt Jess. *Don't forget you're heading out of here come mid-April. No way will Jessica and Nicholas be going with you.*

Jess rocked sideways, regained her balance. Gave him a crooked smile. 'Thanks. I think. Fishing after work would be lovely.' Then she spun round and became very intent on those damned towels again, refolding already neatly folded ones. Shifting them from stack to stack.

'Jackson.' Sheree from Reception popped her head around the corner. 'Mrs Harrop's here to see you.' Her voice dropped several octaves. 'She's not the most patient lady either.'

'On my way.' He stared at Jess's ramrod-straight back, waited for the other woman to return to her desk out front. 'We'll have fish and chips for dinner on the beach. That okay with you? And Nicholas?'

'Sounds great.' Jess turned and he relaxed. Her grin was back. Her eyes were like fudge. 'I'm looking forward to it.'

So was he. A lot. Too much for someone who wasn't getting involved. Face it, taking a woman and her son to do regular stuff like fishing was a first.

'And, Jackson?'

He turned back. 'Yes?'

'Mrs Harrop is a sweetie underneath that grumpy exterior.'

'I'll remember that.' How come Jessica stuck up for the underdog so much? Maybe it was because she'd been the odd one out in those two years she'd been to school here. He'd had the loving, sharing family *and* all the friends at school, and yet he stayed away.

'Mrs Harrop, it's been years since I saw you. Do you even remember me?' Jackson showed the rather large, elderly lady to a chair in the consulting room he was using while Grady was away.

'Could hardly forget the boy who kicked his football through my front window.'

Jackson winced. That had been at least fifteen years ago. He gave Mrs Harrop a rueful smile. 'Sorry about that.'

'You've been away too long, my boy,' she muttered, as she carefully lowered herself onto the seat. 'But you're here now.'

As this was about the fifth time he'd heard almost the exact words since arriving in Golden Bay Jackson didn't react at all. He might even have been disappointed if people hadn't commented on his return, even though it wasn't permanent. After all, since one of his reasons for leaving was that everyone here knew everything about people's business, he'd feel cheated if his actions were no longer justified.

'I wasn't going to miss the wedding. Sasha would

never forgive me.' He wouldn't have forgiven himself. He loved his sister. 'She's so happy, it's wonderful.'

'That Grady was always meant for her.' Mrs Harrop was pulling up her sleeve. 'You going to take my blood pressure, or what?'

'I sure am. But first, how've you been feeling?' He'd read the patient notes before asking Mrs Harrop to come through and knew that she'd had two arterial stents put in six months ago.

'Old, tired, and a lot better than I used to.'

'How's your diet been? Are you sticking to fat-free?' Jackson saw that her last cholesterol test had been a little high but nothing dangerous.

'Your lady makes sure of that.'

'My lady? Mum? Or Sasha?' He wound the cuff of the sphygmomanometer around her upper arm.

'Pssh. I'm talking about Jessica. She's very good to me. Always delivering healthy meals and telling me how she's cooked too much. You'd think she'd have learned a new excuse by now. She's the best neighbour I ever had. Very kind. She genuinely cares about people.'

Alarm bells began clattering in his head. Mrs Harrop was calling Jessica his woman and they'd only spent one night together. Wasn't this why he left Golden Bay in the first place? 'You live in the house next to Jess?' Guess that explained her comment about his woman. At seventy Mrs Harrop might have old fashioned ideas about him spending a night with a lovely young woman.

Without waiting for Mrs Harrop's answer, he stuck the earpieces in and squeezed the bulb to tighten the cuff. Then he listened to the blood pumping through her veins and noted the systolic and diastolic pressures. 'Moderately high. Have you been taking your tablets daily?'

'Yes, young man, I have. But I need a new prescription.' His patient pulled her sleeve down to her wrist and buttoned it. 'She bought both houses.'

'I think you need a different dosage.' Jackson began tapping the computer keyboard. 'She what? Who bought both houses? Jessica?'

Mrs Harrop's chin bobbed up and down, and her eyes lit up with satisfaction. 'Of course, Jessica. She saved my bacon when she bought mine. And now she lets me rent it back for next to nothing. I know I should be paying more but I can't.'

Jackson slumped in his chair. Jess owned both those homes? She hadn't said. *But why should she? She might've talked about her parents earlier but that didn't mean she would be telling you everything. Like you, she can play things close to the chest.* Another vision of that chest flickered through his brain before he had time to stamp on it. Beautiful, full breasts that filled his hands perfectly.

Apparently Mrs Harrop hadn't finished. 'You see, that boy of mine cleaned out my savings and left me with only the house. I wouldn't even have had that if my lawyer hadn't made me get a trustee to oversee any sale I might want to make.'

'I'm sorry to hear that.' But Jess had saved this woman from heartbreak.

'The day Jessica decided to return to Golden Bay was my lucky day.'

'So it would seem.' *Good for you, Jess. You're an absolute star.* Money had never been in short supply in her family, yet she drove a joke of a car and gave her neighbour cheap accommodation. 'Now, Mrs Harrop, here's your prescription. I've upped the dosage a little and I want to see you again next week.'

'Thank you, Doctor. I'll make an appointment on the way out.'

Jess was taking bloods from Gary Hill when he walked back from showing Mrs Harrop out. He asked, 'Hi, Gary. You still into motocross?'

'Gidday, Jackson. Sure am. Though the body's a bit stiff these days and I don't land so easily when I come off. Break a few more bones than I used to.' The guy appeared flushed and lethargic, but had plenty to say. Some things didn't change.

'Maybe it's time to give it up.'

Jess turned to him and rolled her eyes. 'Even when he broke his clavicle and humerus, there was no stopping Gary. You honestly think he'll give up because his body's getting rumpty on him?'

'Guess not.' Jackson was puzzled as to why Jess was taking bloods. 'So what brings you here today? I'm seeing you next, aren't I?'

'I've got a fever. I got malaria last year when I was riding in Malaysia and this feels exactly the same as the previous two bouts.' Gary shrugged. 'Just hope I'm not on my back too long. I'm supposed to be heading away to the Philippines in eight days.'

'Sorry, Jackson, but the courier's due to pick up medical specimens and Roz suggested I take Gary's bloods while he waited to see you.' Jess labelled the tubes of blood for haematology and biochemistry, then made some thick blood smears. Next she stuck a tiny plaster on the needle entry site on Gary's arm. 'There you go. We should hear back tonight about the malaria.'

Back in his room Jackson began to read Gary's file on the computer screen as he asked, 'Any symptoms other than the fever?'

'Hot and cold, hell of a headache, and I keep wanting to toss my food.' Gary eased himself onto a chair, rubbing his left side.

'You're hurting?' Was that his spleen giving him grief, engorged through trying to remove malarial parasites from his blood system?

'That's my old injury from when I came off the bike and broke my pelvis. Still hurts on and off. Guess the arthritis is starting to set in. I was warned.' He yawned deep. 'Yeah, this is familiar. The bone-numbing tired-ness.'

Jackson found a thermometer and slipped it under Gary's tongue. 'Seriously, you ever think about slowing down?' The guy was only thirty-four but at this rate he might not make forty in reasonable working order.

Gary kept his lips sealed around the thermometer and shook his head.

'Fair enough. Your call.' Reading more of the file, he commented, 'I see your malaria was diagnosed as falci-parum. Common in Asia. Had you taken anti-malarials at the time?'

A nod.

Reading the thermometer, he told Gary, 'That's way too high. I hope you've been taking lots of fluids. Let's get you up on the bed so I can check your spleen.'

Jackson gently felt Gary's abdomen. 'Your spleen's definitely enlarged, which fits the diagnosis.'

'Guess I already knew. Can't blame me for hoping I was wrong.'

'When did you start getting symptoms?'

'Started feeling crook night before last, but I was working up the Cobb Valley and wanted to get the job done.'

'You've got to take care of yourself, mate. This ma-laria can be very serious if you stall on getting treatment.'

'I live hard,' Gary growled. 'With my family history

of bowel cancer taking my dad and two brothers, I'm packing in as much as I can in case I'm next.'

It made sense in a way. Jackson asked, 'You married, got kids?'

'Kate Saunders and I got hitched ten years back. Got two youngsters. What about you?'

'No, no kids or wife.'

'What are you waiting for? None of us are getting any younger. You don't want to be in your dotage, with anklebiters hanging on to you.'

'I'll remember you said that.' And try not to think about Jess in the same moment. 'I suggest we get you over the hill to hospital today. I don't want you waiting here until we find out those results. You need intravenous fluids ASAP.'

'Figured you'd say that. Kate's packed my overnight bag.'

He remembered Kate from school, a quiet girl who'd followed the crowd around. After signing a referral to hospital, Jackson went with Gary out to the waiting room and explained everything to Kate. 'It's great to see you both again.'

'You stopping here permanently?' Gary asked.

'No.'

'Why not? I travel a lot but this is the greatest little place on earth.'

Exactly. Little. Too little for him.

Thankfully Jessica joined them and diverted Gary's focus as she handed him a package. 'You might as well take your bloods with you. Save time at the other end, and prevent the need to be jabbed again.'

'Jess, line one for you,' Sheree called. 'It's a Lily Carter.'

'Cool. I hope that means good news on baby Alice Rose.'

'Let me know,' he called after her. That had been their first time working together and he'd enjoyed it.

So far, buster, there hasn't been anything you haven't enjoyed doing with Jess.

Five minutes later the woman swamping his brain popped her head around the door. 'Lily says hi and thank you for everything we did on Sunday. Alice Rose is doing very well and we're getting the credit.' That smile she gave him would get her anything she wanted.

'That's good news. I hated seeing her pain, and I'm not just talking about the labour. She's had more than her share of misfortune.'

'If they have another baby, I don't think Matthew will be taking her far from home. She hated her helicopter flight.'

'What a waste.' He grinned.

A light offshore breeze lifted Jess's hair as she sat on the sand, watching Nicholas trying to fling the fishing line into the water. Unfortunately it kept getting stuck in the sand and seaweed behind him as he threw the rod tip over his shoulder. She chuckled. 'Go slowly with that rod, Nicholas. You don't want to break it.'

'I'm doing what Jackson showed me.'

Right, shut up, Mum, and let the men get on with the job of fishing. 'I guess he knows best.'

'I'm a man, remember. We know these things from birth.' Jackson flicked a cheeky grin her way before carefully lifting the tip of Nicholas's rod out of the sand.

Of course she remembered he was a man. A perfect specimen of a man. Why else had she gone to bed with him? *Because you were so attracted to him you couldn't think straight.* Yeah, well, there was that, too. Which only underlined the fact he was male. She lay back on her towel to soak up some of the end-of-day summer warmth, and glanced at Jackson again.

He was still watching her but now his gaze had dropped to cruise over her scantily clad body. She saw his chest rise and his stomach suck in.

Guess her new bikini was a hit, then. Sasha had told her she would be nuts not to buy it when they'd spent a day in Nelson shopping two weeks ago. While they'd gone for last-minute wedding accessories they'd got side-tracked with lingerie and swimwear for Sasha's honeymoon. Bikinis all round.

Jackson croaked, 'What did I tell you? Orange really suits you.'

'You're close. Burnt orange this time.' Pulling her eyes away from that tantalising view of rock-hard muscles and sexy mouth, she tipped her head back to look up at the sky. Bright blue. The colour of love. Gulp. Her gaze dropped back to the man who'd snatched her heart. Thankfully he was now focused on fishing with Nicholas so she could study him without being caught. Tall, lean and as virile as it was possible to get. Yep, this was definitely love. How fast that had happened. So fast she couldn't trust it. Yet.

Four days after that heady night with him she still didn't know what to do. She'd been surprised when Jackson hadn't taken off at the first hint of her talking about something as personal as her misguided parents. He'd even hugged her, reassured her. Yeah, he wasn't hard to love. Too darned easy, in fact.

'Mummy, something's pulling my line. Look. Mummy, come here, quick. It's jiggling.'

Jackson was holding the rod upright. 'Wind the line in as fast as you can, Nicholas. That's it. Keep it coming. You don't want the fish jumping off the hook.'

'Mummy, look. Is it a fish? Jackson?'

'Yes, sport, you've caught your first fish.' Jackson reached for the hand net on the sand and raced to scoop up the flapping trophy. 'Look at that. Well done, Nicholas. You're a proper fisherman now.'

'Can I see? I want to hold it.' Nicholas dropped the rod and ran at Jackson, who scooped him up and carried boy and net up onto the sand.

'If we tip the fish out here, away from the sea, we won't lose it back in the water.' His long fingers deftly unhooked the ten-centimetre-long herring and handed it to Nicholas. 'Put your fingers where mine are, by the gills. That's it.' In an undertone he added, solely for her benefit, 'I hope you brought the camera, Mum.'

She did an exaggerated eye-roll. 'Would I forget the most important thing?'

After at least ten photos, capturing the biggest smile she'd ever seen on her boy's face, she made Jackson kneel down beside Nicholas and snapped a few more of the pair of happy fishermen. Those would look great in her album. Along with the wedding shots of her and Jackson standing with Sasha and Grady.

'I want to do it again, Jackson.'

'Like a true fisherman.' Jackson retrieved the rod, baited the hook and handed it to Nicholas, then took the herring aside to deal with it.

'Can we have my fish for dinner, Mummy?'

Yuk. Herring. But this was her boy's first fish. 'I guess, but it's very small for three people to share.'

As Nicholas's little face puckered up, ready for an outburst, Jackson saved the moment. 'You know, herrings are usually used for bait to catch bigger fish. Why don't we put it in your mother's freezer for when we go out in the boat after big fish?'

'Okay. What's for dinner? Fishing makes me hungry.'

'Now, there's a surprise.' She blew him a kiss before glancing across to Jackson, who was smiling at Nicholas.

'We're having fish and chips as soon as we've finished fishing, sport. What do you reckon? Had enough with that rod yet?'

'No. I'm going to get another he-herring.'

He did. Two more. Then they packed up and headed to the motor camp and the fast-food shop.

'Fish and chips on the beach in the fading sunlight, with sand for extra texture, and lukewarm cans of soda. I can't think of a better meal,' Jess said an hour later, as she unlocked her front door. Behind her Jackson carried Nicholas from the car.

'Talk about picky. What's wrong with a bit of sand crunching between your teeth?' He grinned. 'Bedroom?'

What a silly question. Of course she wanted to go to her bedroom with him. Her body was leaning towards him like metal to a magnet. That dancing feeling had begun in her stomach.

'Which is Nicholas's room?' Jackson's deep voice interrupted her hot thoughts. A wicked twinkle lightened his eyes.

Oh, yes, Nicholas. She gave herself a mental slap and led the way into the second, smaller bedroom. 'Definitely bedtime for my boy.' He was out for the count, had been all the way home, after talking excitedly nonstop about his fish.

'Whatever else were you thinking?' The bone-melting chuckle played havoc with all her thought processes so that she stood waiting for Jackson to lay Nicholas on the bed.

'Jess? The bedcover?'

Blink. Another mental slap. Concentrate. Heat raced up her cheeks as she hurriedly snatched the quilt out of the way. Then her heart rolled over as Jackson placed Nicholas ever so gently onto his bed and reached for the quilt to tuck it up under his chin. It wouldn't take much for her to get used to this. This was what she wanted for her boy, for herself. Sharing parenthood. Sharing everything.

'Thanks,' she whispered around a thickening in her throat. She found Teddy and slipped him in beside Nicholas, before dropping a kiss on her boy's forehead. She sniffed back her threatening tears, and grinned. 'Yuk. He smells fishy.'

'Only a little.' Jackson draped an arm over her shoulders. 'All part of the fun.'

Sniff, sniff. 'How come you don't reek? You handled those herrings more than Nicholas did.'

'I used the bathroom at the takeaway place. I thought Nicholas had, too.'

'Little boys have to be supervised at cleaning time.' She nudged his ribs with her elbow. 'Want a coffee before you head home?'

His finger touched her chin, tilted her head back so their eyes met. 'Any chance I can stay longer than a coffee?'

She melted against him. 'Every chance.'

'What's this?' Jess's fingers were running over Jackson's flat belly, seeking pleasure, hopefully giving pleasure, as they lay luxuriating in the aftermath of great sex.

Under her hand he stilled. 'An old wound.'

Didn't feel that old to her. The scar was still soft with a rough ridge running through the puckered skin. 'Define old.' If he refused to answer she'd back off. Everyone was entitled to privacy.

'Five weeks.'

'That is a long time.' She smiled into the dark.

'Seems like yesterday.' He rolled onto his side and ran a finger from her shoulder down to her breast, flicked across the nipple, sending shards of hot need slicing through her.

Okay, so this was the sidetrack trick. She'd run with it. She might be missing out on something important but amazing sex wasn't a bad second.

Then Jackson said, 'I was knifed.'

'What?' She bolted upright and stared down at him in the half-light from the hall. A low-wattage light always ran in case Nicholas woke up needing the bathroom. 'You must've really annoyed someone.'

'Come back down here.' He reached and tugged at her until she complied, sliding down the bed and finishing up tucked in against him. 'You don't want to know.'

'Wrong, Jackson. I do.'

She felt his chest lift as he drew a breath. Then he told her. 'In Hong Kong there's a group of doctors and nurses I belong to outside the hospital. We look after the poor and underprivileged during the hours of darkness. We mostly visit night shelters but occasionally the police call us to look at someone who refuses to get help.'

'You do this as well as work in the emergency department of a large hospital?' No wonder the guy looked exhausted most of the time. 'This is what you were referring to the other night when I asked why you were so tired.'

'Not quite.' He leaned in and dropped the softest of kisses on the corner of her mouth. Then he lay on his back, hands behind his head, and stared up at the ceiling. 'It was Christmas Eve. Fireworks displays out on the harbour. Plenty of tourists and locals enjoying themselves.'

Jess wound an arm over his waist and laid her cheek on his chest. 'Lots of booze.'

'Lots and lots of booze.' Jackson was quiet for a long time. Under her cheek she could feel his heart thudding. Tension had crept into his body. Her hand softly massaged his thigh. Finally, he said, 'The unit I worked with was doing the rounds of the usual haunts when we had a call from the police to meet them three streets over where they'd found a woman claiming she'd been raped.'

Running her fingers back and forth over his skin, Jess waited. He'd tell his tale in his own time, and she had all night.

'It was a set-up. We were attacked the moment we turned the corner. The nurse with me...' His Adam's apple bobbed. 'It should've been me, not Juliet who got the fatal blow. But she was always a fast sprinter.'

'Your friend ran into the attackers?'

'Slap bang onto the knives they wielded.'

'So you feel guilty because you didn't take the hit.' Her hand smoothed over those tense muscles. 'How were you to know that would happen?' About now he'd go all silent on her. 'Is this why you get angry at times?'

'Yeah.'

She waited quietly, only her hand moving as it swept his skin.

Exhaling, he continued. 'Frustration, guilt, vulnerability all add up to an ugly picture. It's debilitating.'

It took a brave man to tell her that. She wrapped herself around him, held him tight. Just listened.

'She didn't make it. I tried. Believe me, I did everything in my power to save her. But she'd been struck in the heart. There was absolutely nothing I could do but wait for the ambulance, hold her hand and keep talking. Noting the things she wanted me to tell her family, dreading that I might forget even one little detail.'

'She knew she was dying.'

'Yeah.' His sigh was so sad it tugged at her heart. 'I couldn't hide that from her. She was too experienced in emergency medicine.'

'You were wounded, too.'

'Yeah. But I survived.'

With one hand she traced the outline of the scar that ran down his thigh. 'Why did they attack you?'

'No one knows. So far the men who did this haven't been found. The police put every resource they had into finding them but no one's talking. The cops don't think it was personal, in that it wasn't me or Juliet they were targeting but more likely the organisation we worked for.'

'Will you continue with that when you return to Hong Kong?'

'Juliet made me promise not to give up our work on the streets because of this.'

That was a big ask. Jess chilled. No wonder Jackson wasn't staying in Golden Bay. He believed he had to go back even if he didn't want to. That promise would be strong, hanging over him, adding to his guilt if he even considered not returning. 'She didn't say not to quit if you had other compelling reasons.' *Like your mum. Like me.*

'I think I need to go back, if only to get past what happened. I don't mind admitting I'll be scared witless the first time I hit the streets, probably see knife-wielding attackers at every dark corner. At the same time I find myself wondering what it would be like to create a life outside medicine.'

Jess caught her breath. What sort of life? Where? Breathing out, she admitted her disappointment. He hadn't said he intended changing hospitals or countries. 'Guess you've got time to make that decision.'

'True. Doesn't get any easier, though. I don't know if

I'm reacting to the attack or if I'm genuinely ready for a change.'

Her hands began moving up his sides, lightly touching his skin, gentling the tension gripping him. Her lips kissed his chest, found a nipple and she began to lick slowly, teasing him to forget the pain of that night. Gradually his reaction changed from tension caused by his story to a tension of another kind, pushing into her thigh. Shifting slightly so that she held him between her thighs, she slid a hand between them and began to rub that hard evidence of his need.

'Jessica,' he groaned through clenched teeth. 'Please don't stop. I need this. I need *you*.'

She had no intention of stopping. Not when her libido was screaming for release. She had to have him—deep inside her.

Suddenly she was flipped onto her back. Jackson separated her thighs to kneel between them. His hands lifted her backside and then he drove into her. Withdrew. Forged forward. Withdrew. And her mind went blank as her body was swamped with heat and desire and need.

CHAPTER SIX

A VOICE CUT through Jess's dreams, dragging her cotton-wool-filled mind into the daylight. 'Who—?'

'Now for the seven o'clock news. Last night—'

The radio alarm. She shut the annoying drone out, concentrated on why she felt so languid this morning. 'Jackson.' Why else? Who else?

Rolling her head sideways, she saw what she already knew. He'd gone. Sneaked out some time in the early hours while she'd been snoozing, gathering her energy around her. For another round of exquisite sex? Turning to glance the other way, she smiled. A note lay on the bedside table.

'Didn't want to be around when Nicholas woke in case it caused trouble. See you at the medical centre. Hugs, J.'

Thoughtful as well as sexy. Great combination, Jackson. And I still love you. But you are going away again and I can understand why. Unfortunately.

Leaping out of bed, she tugged the curtains open. Yep, the sky was as blue as the lightest sapphire. The colour of love. Love meant letting go and waiting for him to come back.

'Now for the weather forecast.' Behind her the voice droned on. 'Expect showers this morning and if you're thinking of going out on the briny, maybe you should find something else to do. Forty-knot northerlies are predicted from around lunchtime.'

Showers? The day was light and sunny. 'Get a new forecast, buddy.' She clicked the pessimist off and headed for the shower.

Twenty minutes later Nicholas bounced into the kitchen and pulled out a chair at the table. 'I want cocoa pops.'

'Please,' Jess said. Placing the bowl and box of cereal on the table, she did a double take. 'What are you wearing?'

'My fishing shirt. This is the lucky shirt. Jackson told me I should wear it every time I go fishing with him.'

So there were to be more fishing expeditions? 'That's fine, but you're going to play centre this morning, not fishing. Take it off and put it in the washing basket.'

'No. I'm wearing it so my friends can see it.' The cocoa pops overflowed from the bowl onto the table. 'I'm going to tell them all about the three fishes I got.'

Removing the carton from Nicholas's hand, she put it back in the cupboard, out of reach. 'That's more than enough cereal. Let's put half those pops in another bowl before you add the milk or there'll be a big mess.'

Too late. The puffed rice spilled over the rim on a tide of milk. 'Whoa, stop pouring now.' She snatched the milk container away.

'I want more milk.' Nicholas banged his spoon on the tabletop. 'More milk, more milk.'

'Sorry, buddy, but you've got more than enough.' She spooned coffee granules into a mug, added half a teaspoon extra, then two sugars. As she dropped two slices of wholegrain in the toaster the front doorbell rang.

Behind her a chair slammed back against the wall. 'I'll get it.' Nicholas raced out of the kitchen.

'Hello, Mr Fisherman.' A deep, sexy voice echoed down the hallway before Jess had made it to the kitchen doorway. Her stomach turned to mush as she peeped around the doorframe and drank in the sight of this man who seemed to hold her heart in his hand.

'Mummy, it's Jackson,' Nicholas yelled, as though she was already at the medical centre.

'Morning.' Jackson had somehow moved along the hall to stand in front of her. 'You're looking good enough to eat this morning.'

Corny. But nice. 'Want a coffee?'

'Please, ta.'

Nicholas jumped up and down in front of Jackson. 'I'm wearing my fishing shirt. See?'

Jackson flicked a question her way. 'Not your idea?'

She shook her head.

'See, here's the thing, Nicholas. Fishing shirts are special and we men have got to look after them. They need washing after you've caught fish, and then put away in the drawer until next time you go to the beach.'

Nicholas was nodding solemnly. 'Okay. I'll go and change.'

Jess stared after Nicholas as he sped out of the room. 'How did you do that? I could spend ten minutes arguing myself blue in the face about that shirt and he'd still wear it to play centre.'

'Hey. Solo parenting can't be so easy. You've got to make all the calls.' A friendly arm encircled her shoulders, tugged her in against a warm, strong body. 'From what I saw last night, you have a good relationship with Nicholas. Don't be so hard on yourself. It's not like you have family here to support you or give you a break.'

The more she got to know Jackson the more talkative

he got. 'Thanks.' Reluctantly she pulled out of his hold. 'Have you had breakfast?'

'Toast on the run. Sam's sheep got into Mum's orchard overnight. I helped Kevin round them up and get them back in their rightful paddock.'

'Kevin's turning out to be very helpful.'

'Where'd he come from?'

Jess handed him a coffee as she answered. 'He and Tamara had an unexpected baby, which Sasha and Grady delivered. There are some terrible family issues involving Tamara's family. Seems the young couple got so much help when the locals heard about the baby and every-thing else that they decided to stay here. Your dad offered Kevin work on the orchard, helping Virginia, and since Sam's accident he hasn't been able to go back to driving full time so Kevin fills in for him as needed.'

'That's why they're living in the orchard cottage.'

'Yep. Sasha moved in with Grady after Melanie was born. Kevin and Tamara needed somewhere to stay. Sim-ple.'

'Is this shirt okay, Jackson?' Nicholas bounded back and climbed onto his chair.

After silently checking with her, Jackson gave his ap-proval. 'You'd better get on with your breakfast, sport. It's nearly time to go to play group.'

Jess held her breath. But the kitchen became quiet ex-cept for the steady munching of cocoa pops. She shook her head and turned to Jackson. 'That's a turnaround. You sure you're not staying for good?'

His smile faltered then returned. 'Can I take a rain-check?'

Her eyes must have been out on stalks. They'd cer-tainly widened so that they were stretching. Her mouth dried. As she stared at Jackson he shoved a hand through his hair, mussing it nicely.

'You are making it so tempting, believe me.' His chest rose. 'But I have to be very honest here. I can't see me staying. For a start, there isn't an emergency department for me to find work at.'

'There's one two hours away over the hill.'

His lips pressed together and she knew she'd gone too far. But this wasn't a one-sided conversation. Was it?

'Like I've already explained, I don't see myself settling back into such a small community. I didn't much like it the first time round.' His chest rose and fell. 'Not to mention my promise to Juliet.'

She couldn't complain that he hadn't given her the facts. He was more honest than she was. But she had no intention of telling him she'd fallen in love with him. Not when she knew deep down she couldn't start a serious relationship. Her son was more important than her love for any man. So that meant keeping her mouth shut and enjoying whatever happened between her and Jackson. 'Thank you for being honest.'

'Jess,' he called softly. 'Am I asking too much if I say I'd like to carry on with what we've got? Is that selfish?'

'It would only be selfish if you were the only one getting something out of it.' Even to her, the smile she made felt lacklustre. Trying again, she came up with something stronger, warmer. 'I…' I'm stuck for words.

'It's okay. You don't have to say anything.'

But I do. I want to. 'Until Saturday night I never expected to meet a man I'd feel so relaxed and comfortable with. You touch something within me, and—' Oh hell, why wasn't this easy? Maybe she should come out with it, tell him she loved him. Except she had to remember that she carried her parents' genes—she would never be able to trust herself to be a good parent when she was in love with someone else. Mum and Dad were devoted to each other, to the point she'd always felt like a spare part in their lives. She'd never do that to Nicholas. 'Jackson, you're special and you make me feel the same way. So, yes, let's carry on with whatever it is we've got.'

Did that sound like a business arrangement? Nah, who had hot sex with their business partner? She started to giggle. This really was an oddball situation, and she had no intention of dropping it. Her giggles turned to laughter.

'What's funny, Mummy?' Nicholas tapped Jackson on the arm. 'Mummy doesn't like laughing.'

Jackson's eyes widened. 'Must be my fault. She laughs a lot around me.'

'That's because you're funny,' Nicholas told him as he got down from the table.

'Funny ha-ha or funny strange? No, don't answer that, either of you.' Jackson grinned at her boy.

'Funny cool.' Getting herself under control, Jess noticed Nicholas heading for his bedroom. 'Nicholas, come back and put your bowl and spoon in the sink, please.'

'You do it. I'm getting my school bag.'

'Nicholas. Do as I say. Please.'

'No. Too busy.'

Jackson glanced at her then down the hall. 'Hey, sport, that's not the way for a boy to talk to his mother. Better come and do as she says.'

She held her breath, and waited through the sudden silence that descended on her home.

'Okay, coming,' her son called, moments before he bounced back into the kitchen. There was the clatter of his plate dropping in the sink, followed by the spoon.

Then he snatched up the cloth and wiped the spilled milk further across the table. 'There, Mummy, all clean.'

Jess rescued the cloth from sliding off the edge of the bench and rinsed it under the tap. 'Thanks, Nicholas. You can finish getting ready for play group now.' As she re-wiped the table she didn't know whether to be pleased or unhappy at Jackson's help. He'd certainly got a good response from Nicholas. Far more than she'd managed. 'Thank you,' she whispered.

'Like I said, you're a good mum, Jessica Baxter. You're too hard on yourself.' Those arms she was coming to rely on for comfort were winding around her again.

Sighing she pulled back and looked up into those green eyes that reminded her of spring and new growth. New love? Don't think like that. Some time soon Jackson will twig what you're thinking and then where will you be? Out in the cold. 'Guess we'd better get cracking. The centre opens in fifteen and I've got antenatal clinic this morning.'

At the medical centre Jackson sat at the staff kitchen table, a strong, long black coffee in hand, and listened to Roz and Rory discussing their patients. 'Seems there's no end of people needing lots of care.'

Jess hadn't had a moment to spare during the day. Mike was at home, catching up on sleep after a night up on Takaka Hill helping Search and Rescue haul a caver out of Harwood's Hole. The man had slipped and fallen fifty metres, breaking both legs on landing at the bottom.

Rory told him, 'Summer is always busier. The influx of holidaymakers adds to our workload something ter-rible. Not to mention numerous cavers and trampers get-ting out into the wilderness.'

Roz added, 'It's as if people leave the cautious side of
their brains at home when they pack to go on holiday.'

'You must remember what it was like when you were
growing up here, Jackson,' Rory said.

'Sure, but I wasn't a doctor. I got to see a few incidents
that occurred amongst my mates. I don't remember anything too serious happening.'

'What about when those guys took a dinghy out with
too big a motor for the size of the boat? They flipped the
boat and nearly drowned themselves. Saved by another
boat going past. And by you swimming out to rescue one
of them. He would've drowned if it hadn't been for you
and the doctor on board the second boat.'

When had Jess come into the room? When had his an-
tennae failed him? He always knew when she was within
metres of him. Or so he'd thought. 'Ben and Haydon.
Damned idiots they were.'

'Lucky idiots, by the sound of it.' Rory picked up a
printout of a lab result. 'I see it's confirmed Gary's got
another bout of falciparum. We need to look into what
else can be down to prevent further attacks. Jackson, do
you see much malaria in Hong Kong?'

'We get quite a few patients presenting but then they're
passed on to the medical team and that's it as far as the
emergency department is concerned. But I can give you
a contact at the hospital if you like.'

From under lowered eyelids he watched Jess as she
filled her water bottle. The movement of leaning slightly
forward over the sink accentuated her sweet curves, especially that butt he'd cupped in his hands last night.
His mouth dried while below his belt muscles stirred.
Was there such a thing as having too much of Jess? Not
in this lifetime.

'Have you got many house calls, Jess?' Rory asked.

'Five for this afternoon, which isn't too bad. I'll stop by and see Claire Johnston and baby Max on my way home.'

Jackson sat up straighter. 'I'll give you another prescription for antibiotics for Max. Talking to Claire earlier, she said the baby still has a wheezy cough.'

Jess gave him one of those heart-melting smiles of hers. 'Sure. Send it through to the pharmacy and I'll pick it up on my way.' She pulled a pen from her pocket and scribbled a note on the back of her hand. 'There, shouldn't forget now.'

'Right.' Roz pushed her chair back and stood up. 'Might as well get this show on the road.'

Rory stayed seated, twirling his mug back and forth in his hands, like he was waiting for the others to disappear.

'Baby Carrington's due any day now so I'll be hovering.' Jess shoved her water bottle in the fridge and followed Roz.

Jackson drained his coffee and stood up. 'You want to say something?' he asked Rory.

The mug kept moving back and forth in those big hands resting on the table. 'Are you fixed on returning to Hong Kong at the end of your leave?'

'Definitely. Nothing to keep me here.' Why did an image of a pair of all-seeing, fudge-coloured eyes suddenly dance across his brain?

'Pity.' Rory lifted his gaze from the table to Jackson. 'Will you go back to working on the streets at night?'

How did he know about that? 'Of course. There's no end of work out there.'

'Your near-miss with a knife hasn't changed your attitude?'

Disappointment was a hard ball in the pit of his gut. 'Jess has been talking too much.' So the very thing that had made him wary about being here had come back to haunt him—in less than three weeks.

Rory's eyebrows lifted. 'Jess?' Then understanding dawned. 'Not Jess. Dr Ng Ping.'

What was going on here? Ping was his department head, and probably the closest he had to a friend in Hong Kong. Why had he and Rory been in touch? 'You care to explain?' Jackson's blood started to simmer. If anyone had anything to say about him, they should say it to his face.

'Dr Ng rang to ask after your health. Said whenever he talked to you, you only ever told him you were fine.'

'Wait until I see Ping. He had no right to do that.' The simmer was becoming a boil. How could Ping do that behind his back? He, more than most, understood how important it was to him to be above board in everything.

'He told me he was a concerned friend who wanted to know you were doing as well as you said. That you are getting over the incident.'

Had Ping told Rory about his meltdown in the middle of the department one particularly busy night? Yes, Jackson would bet everything he owned on it. Pulling out a chair, he straddled it and eyeballed Rory. 'I still have small temper surges at the most unexpected moments, but they disappear quickly, and they happen less and less often. Nothing has happened here at the centre, and no patients have any reason to be concerned. Neither do you and your partners.' Bile soured his mouth. And he'd been stupid enough to think loose-tongued people only lived in Golden Bay.

'Relax, Jackson. I have absolutely no qualms about you working with us. No one else knows about that call either. I figured it wasn't necessary.'

'So where's this headed? I'm sure the waiting room is

bursting with people wanting our services.' The threatening temper outburst backed off a little.

Rory got up and shut the door, came back to the table but didn't sit. 'I'm getting antsy, want to head home to Auckland. But my conscience won't let me leave these guys in the lurch. Not before I've tried all avenues I can think of to find a replacement.'

Jackson stared at him. 'You're asking if I want to stay on permanently?' Of course, the man knew next to nothing about him and how he'd left the moment the school bell had rung for the last time on his school life. Hell. How had his parents coped with that? He'd never stopped to ask. Maybe he should. *Only if you can handle the answer.*

'Yeah, something like that.' Rory grimaced. 'Your face tells me all I need to know. But if Jess manages to change your mind, let me know, will you?'

Jackson felt his mouth drop open. Was it really that obvious? Guess so if Rory had noticed. *Grady, the sooner you're home the better for me. And as for Ping—I'm ringing you tonight. Pal.*

His stomach tightened and his hands balled into fists as his head spun. Damn you, Ping. Thankfully Rory had disappeared out the door without seeing this tantrum.

'Hey, what's up? You look ready to shoot someone.' Jess was back. Her hand gripped his shoulder, shook him softly.

'My so-called friend in Hong Kong has been checking up on me. Rory took a call from Ping and now knows about the attack.'

Jess smiled. Smiled? This was serious.

'Jackson, friends do that. This Ping obviously cares about you, wants to make sure you're doing okay.' Her mouth came close, caressed his cheek with the lightest of kisses. 'He's doing the right thing.'

And just like that, the tension disappeared. The anger evaporated. His arms encircled this wonderful woman. 'You are so good for me.' And he kissed her, thoroughly. Until there was a knock on the door.

'Mind if I get a coffee?' Sheree asked.

Jess leapt back and winked at him. 'Just leaving.'

In his consulting room Jackson studied the notes of his first patient for the day. Dawn Sullivan, thirty-nine years old, no major health issues during the five years she'd been coming to the Golden Bay Medical and Wellbeing Centre.

He turned to study the woman sitting opposite. Her cheeks appeared unnaturally pale. 'So, Dawn, what brings you to see me today?'

'I'm so tired all the time I can hardly get out of bed some days. I've got the attention span of a fly, which is great considering school started this week and I'm a teacher.' Even as she spoke Dawn was yawning.

'You don't have any history of anaemia. How are your periods? Heavier than usual? Or do they last longer these days?'

Shaking her head, his patient told him, 'All much the same as ever. But I do get lots of stomachaches. Actually, I ache everywhere at times. It's like I've got the flu full time. I'd planned on finally painting my house over the summer break but hardly got one wall done I've been that short of energy. Not like me at all. Ask anyone around here. I always used to be on the go.'

'How long has this been going on?' he asked.

Dawn looked sheepish. 'Months. At first I went to the naturopath, who gave me vitamins and minerals. Fat lot of good they turned out to be and nearly bankrupted me in the process. Whatever I've got is getting worse. I've lost a bit of weight, which normally would make me happy but right now worries me sick.'

Jackson felt as though he should be sitting in the back of a classroom as Dawn's voice carried loudly across the small gap between them. He read Dawn's blood pressure—normal; checked her eyes—they showed signs of anaemia. 'Can you get up on the bed and I'll examine your abdomen.' After a few moments of gently pressing over the area he stepped back. 'I can't feel anything out of the ordinary.'

'So what do you think is going on?' Dawn sat up and pulled her top back into place.

'I'd say you're anaemic but the cause needs to be checked out. We'll do some blood tests. Any changes in diet? Or are you a vegan?'

Dawn shuddered. 'No, love my meat too much for that.'

'We'll start with these blood tests.' He glanced at the patient notes on his computer screen. Something was bothering him. 'Your house is going to have to wait a little longer for its new coat.'

'Right now I'd be happy to have enough energy to teach all day.'

Jackson tapped his forefinger on the desktop. Checking Dawn's address, he tried to remember the style of houses in that road. 'Your house—how old is it?'

'About seventy years. It's a bungalow. The wide boards and wooden window frames type. Mighty cold in winter.'

'Did you do a lot of preparation for the paint job? Sanding off old paint, for example?'

'Yes, I spent weeks with an electric sander, getting down to bare boards. From what I could see, it hadn't been done properly in for ever.'

Bingo. 'I might be wrong but I have a hunch that what you're suffering from is lead poisoning. The old paints are notorious for having a lead component. Did you wear a mask while you were using the sander?'

'No. I can get lead from inhaling dust granules?' Dawn sank down onto the chair, looking shocked. 'It's bad, isn't it? Lead poisoning? Really?'

The more he thought about it the more certain he was. On the screen he ticked boxes on the laboratory form. 'We won't know for sure until the haematology results come back but I think we're onto something. So let's forget those vitamins and wait for a couple of days. If you do have lead in your system, it has to be removed by chelation therapy.'

'Meaning?' Dawn's voice had grown smaller, no longer the booming teacher's tone.

'You'd be given chelation agents that absorb the lead from your body tissues, which is then passed out through your urine. It's an effective way for cleaning up the lead and then we can treat the residual effects, like that lack of energy, which will be due to an anaemia caused by the poisoning.' Signing the form, he added, 'Take this through to Jess. I don't think she's left for her rounds yet.'

'Thank you, Doctor.'

'It's Jackson, and I'll phone you as soon as the results come through.'

'Again, thank you. Guess this means the house and my job are on hold.'

'Talk to the school board and see if you can take on reduced hours for this term.' He held the door open and ushered Dawn through, before going in search of his next patient.

Kelly Brown walked carefully and slowly into his room and eased her bottom onto the edge of the chair.

Her face, arms and every other bit of exposed skin was the colour of well-ripened tomatoes. She wore a loose dress that barely reached her thighs and probably had nothing on underneath.

Jackson sat down and said, 'You're here for that sunburn?'

Kelly nodded. 'It's awful. Can you do anything to stop the heat? Or the pain? I can't wear clothes or lie under the sheet. It hurts all the time.'

'I'll give you a mild painkiller. I hope you're drinking lots of water.'

'Mum nags at me all the time.' Kelly moved, grimaced.

'Where did you get so much sun? It was overcast here yesterday.' Or so he'd thought.

'A group of us went over the hill to Kaiteriteri Beach. Everyone got a bit of sunburn but nothing like this.'

Jackson typed up details on her notes. 'Do you have naturally fair skin?' When she nodded he added, 'You should know better, then. Lots of sunscreen all the time. Any blisters?'

'On my back and all down the front. I've always been sort of careful but yesterday I forgot to take the sunblock with me and thought I'd be safe if I got out of the sun after an hour. But I fell asleep sunbathing.'

'Cool showers, lots of fluids and a mild analgesic is all I can recommend, Kelly. And stay out of the sun in future.'

Taking the prescription he handed her, she said, 'Think I'll move to Alaska. Should be safe there.'

He laughed. 'Might be eaten by a bear.'

'At least that'd be different.' Kelly hobbled to the door. 'Thanks, Doctor. I hear you're only here while Grady's away. Can you tell Jess I won't be able to babysit this week?'

'Your cellphone not working?' Why the hell did this teen think he should be passing Jess her messages?

'Nothing wrong with it. Thought you might like an excuse to talk to her.' With a cheeky wink the minx left his room.

Jackson stared after her. Small towns. There was no getting away from the fact everyone knew everyone's business. How many weeks before he caught the big tin bird back to Asia? Too many.

Then he thought of the woman he was supposed to pass Kelly's message on to and took back that thought. Not nearly enough days left.

CHAPTER SEVEN

JESS HELD BABY Carrington while his mother wriggled herself into a comfortable position on the bed.

'Is this going to be hard? Painful?' Anna asked, anxiety in her voice, as she reached for her baby.

'No and no.' Jess carefully placed the baby in Anna's arms. 'But remember I told you your milk mightn't come in for the first few days. You'll most likely be feeding him colostrum, which is full of goodies he needs.'

'How do I hold him? Oh, hello, gorgeous. Aren't you the most beautiful baby ever?' Anna beamed as she studied her son.

'He's a little cracker, absolutely beautiful.' As they all were. When Nicholas had been placed in her arms for the very first time she couldn't believe her overwhelming sense of love for her son. She'd seen exactly the same reaction in every mother she'd delivered before and since Nicholas's birth, only nowadays she understood how deep the bond ran. How it was the start of something that stayed with mothers for the rest of their lives. Life-changing, empowering. Frightening.

Anna finally raised her gaze. 'Show me how to hold him so I can feed him.'

Tucking the baby in against Anna so she supported his shoulders, Jess then placed Anna's hand on his head.

'Holding him like that means he can access your nipple easily. That's it. Now rub his mouth against your nipple to encourage him to suck. That's it. Perfect.'

'Wow, that's awesome. Oh, my goodness, I'm feeding my baby.' Anna's eyes grew misty. 'Danny, look at this.'

The baby's father was transfixed, watching his son. A bemused expression covered his face. 'That's amazing.'

Jess felt a similar sense of wonder. This was always a wonderful sight, mum bonding with baby. Memories of Nicholas tugged at her heart again. *I'd love to do it all over again. Have a brother or sister for Nicholas.* And where on earth had that idea come from?

Jackson. Of course. Loving him had sparked all sorts of weird ideas. Ideas she wouldn't follow through on. Nicholas needed all her attention. It wouldn't be fair to expect him to share her with Jackson. *What about that baby you suddenly want? Can you spread your love between two children without depriving one or the other?* Surely that would be different? A mother's love was very different from the love she felt for Jackson.

Besides, it was one thing to find herself a solo mother of one, but of two? That would be plain irresponsible. Jackson wouldn't be staying, baby or no baby. That was unfair. He was a very responsible man. But she wouldn't be wanting a loveless—make that one-sided—relationship.

Anna's question cut through her turmoil. 'How will I know when he's hungry?'

Jess dragged up a smile. 'Believe me, he'll let you know. His lungs are in good working order.'

Danny grinned. 'Just like his dad.'

'I feel so much happier now that I've tried feeding him. It isn't the nightmare I'd thought it might be.' Anna gazed adoringly at the baby. 'He's looking sleepy.'

'Carefully take him off your breast. You need to wind

him now. Place him on your shoulder and rub his back gently. That's it. You're a natural at this.'

'Who'd have believed it, huh? It's not like my day job as a gardener gave me any clues.'

'I'm going to leave you two to get to know your son. What are you naming him, by the way?'

'Antony.'

'Michael.'

Jess grinned. 'Right, you definitely need to sort that out. Call the nurse if you have any problems with any-thing, otherwise I'll be in to see you later.'

She went to find Sheryl and hand over her patient. 'I'm off. I doubt you'll be needing me, though I'll drop by later. That baby might've been two weeks late but the birth was straightforward and Anna's already man-aging feeding.'

Sheryl waved her out the door. 'Go and enjoy the weekend. It's a stunner of a day.'

It certainly was. Summer had turned on its absolute best for the weekend, which had brought people in droves from Nelson and other towns to their beach houses. At home Jess stood on her deck with a glass of icy water and looked around. Bright blue skies—the colour of love—sparkled above and not a whisper of wind stirred the leaves on the trees in the neighbour's yard. The sparrows and finches were singing while the tuis were squabbling over the last few yellow flowers of a kowhai tree.

'Mummy, can I go swimming at the beach?'

'After lunch has settled in your tummy I'll take you down to Pohara.' She'd picked him up from Bobby's on the way home. Studying him now, that feeling of awe that had struck her as she'd watched Anna and her baby bonding returned in full force.

Was Nicholas missing out because he didn't have a sibling? When she'd been young she'd pestered her mother about why she didn't have a sister like her friends did. Her mother had always told her that she got more love being the only one but somehow that had never washed with Jess. There hadn't been much love. She'd grown up fast, only having adults around to talk to most of the time. She hadn't spent a lot of time in places where there were other kids for her to play with.

'Why can't Jackson come with me?' Nicholas rode his bike round and round the lemon tree, making her feel dizzy watching him.

'He's busy picking the avocados for Virginia.' Nicholas definitely missed out by not having a father. Balancing that against what he'd miss out on if the man she loved lived with them, she suddenly didn't know what was best for them all.

'Actually, I've finished that chore,' a familiar deep voice said from the corner of the house. 'Got up with the birds to do the picking. I've even graded and packed the avocados, ready to go to the markets.'

'Jackson, look at me,' Nicholas shouted, and pedalled faster than ever until he forgot to watch where he was going and rode into the lemon tree.

Jess winced and rushed to lift him back onto his bike. 'Nicholas, be careful, sweetheart.'

'Okay, Mummy.'

Jackson moved up beside her. 'Hey, you're looking great.' Sex oozed from that voice, lifting bumps on her skin.

'Go easy around you know who,' she warned, at the same time noticing how his gaze cruised over her legs. She'd pulled on very short shorts and a singlet top the moment she'd got home, feeling the need to make the most of the sun after hours shut inside that small delivery room. 'Anna Carrington had her baby this morning.'

Jackson's eyes softened. 'So you've been up most of the night?'

'All of it.'

'You don't look like you're wilting.' He ran a finger down her arm. 'What did she have?'

'A boy.' She couldn't help the sigh that slid across her lips.

'That cute, eh?'

'Yes. I never get tired of seeing new babies.'

'You sound as though you're yearning for another of your own.' Jackson's finger hovered over her wrist.

Her feelings were too obvious if Jackson was picking up on them. 'It's easy to wish for another baby when they're brand-new and behaving and I'm not at home alone trying to balance everything like a one-winged bird.'

Jackson turned to stare across her lawn, his eyes following Nicholas as he again rode faster and faster, happily showing off. 'You'd have to choose a father.'

She sucked in a breath. Odd way of putting it. 'Not doing that. I do not want to have another child on my own, no matter how cool it would be for Nicholas to have a sibling. It's not fair on the children.'

'Or you. It's hard work, for sure.' He still watched Nicholas, but what was going on in his head?

'It's not about the hard work. It's about having two role models, a male perspective as well as mine. Anyway, I don't know why we're having this conversation. It's not going to happen.'

Jackson turned then, his hands reaching for her arms. 'You sound so certain.'

Because I am. Because you're going away. Because I

couldn't trust myself not to be able to share my love be-tween you and Nicholas and any other child even if you did stay. 'I'm being practical. No point wishing for the impossible. Takes too much energy.' She stepped back, pulling her arms free. 'Want to go to the beach with us?'

Disappointment blinked out at her. 'You're changing the subject.'

'Are you staying on in Golden Bay come April?'

He hesitated, and she held her breath. Until, 'No.'

Now it was her turn to feel disappointed, despite knowing the answer before he'd enunciated it. Swallowing hard, she said, 'Then of course I'm changing the subject. We're going to the beach. Want to join us?'

'Yes, Jackson, you've got to come.' Nicholas let rip with another shout as he spun around on his bike too fast and tipped over. 'I want you to,' he yelled, through the too-long grass covering his face.

'How can I refuse that demand?' Jackson shrugged in her direction, puzzlement in his eyes. So he'd picked up on what she hadn't said. That she'd be interested if he was hanging around.

'I guess Nicholas has a way with words.' If only it was that easy for her to get Jackson to do what she needed. Because it was slowly dawning on her that she wasn't going to be able to let him go as easily as she'd first thought. For a moment there she'd almost wished he'd said he was staying and that they might make their relationship more permanent. For a moment she thought she could see past her fears and take a chance. For a moment.

Jackson went to right the bike and held it while Nicholas climbed back on. 'You're going to need a bigger bike soon.'

'I told Mummy but she said I had to wait.'

A bigger bike meant further to fall. 'There's no hurry.'

'Have you got sun block on, sport?'

'Yes.' Nicholas nodded gravely. 'Kelly got burnt at the beach. She said it hurt a lot.'

'That's right, she was bright red. You don't want to look like a fried tomato.'

Jess watched the two of them: Jackson so patient and Nicholas so keen to show off his skills. They looked good together. If only this relationship could last as it was, but the weeks were cranking along, disappearing unbelievably fast. The first of March was only a couple of days away, and that heralded the end of summer. Then it would be April and some time during that month it would be the end of her affair with Jackson. Swallowing down on the sudden sadness engulfing her, she vowed to make the most of whatever time she had with him. For someone who did not want a permanent relationship with any man she was making a right hash of keeping Jackson at arm's length.

'You're daydreaming again.' Jackson stood in front of her.

'Must be the heat.' She poured the last of her water down her throat.

'Shucks. Here I was thinking I might be the reason you had that far-away look in your eye.'

'Nope. That was pollen from the lemon flowers.'

His finger ran along her bottom lip, sending zips of heat right down to her toes. 'Is that why you always smell of citrus? You spend a lot of time hauling Nicholas out of the lemon tree?'

Rising onto her toes, she nudged his hand out of the way and kissed those full, sexy lips that knew how to tease and tantalise her for hours on end. 'Try reading the label of my shampoo bottle. Less exotic but more practical.'

He took over the kiss, deepening it until she had to hang on to keep her balance. Pressing her body up against his, she felt the hardening of his reaction to her. Not now. Not here. Hands on his chest, she pushed back. 'Nicholas.'

His sultry eyes widened. 'God, I'm like a crazed teen around you, forgetting everything except what you make me feel, want.' Jackson stepped back, tugged at his shirt to cover the obvious reaction to their kiss. 'Better do something else before the trouble really starts.'

'I'll get towels and things for the beach.' How mundane was that? It should dampen their ardour.

Jackson followed her inside. 'I came around to ask you what you think about camping.'

'As in a tent? Sleeping bags and air mattresses? That sort of camping?' It had been years since she'd done that and then it had been in the Australian outback with her parents. She'd spent her whole time sitting up with the thin sleeping bag zipped right to her throat, terrified a snake would come into her tent and bite her.

'Is there any other sort?' Jackson grinned. 'A friend from way back has a bit of land by the beach out at Wainui Inlet. There's a shed with bathroom and cooking facilities. I figured we could go out there and pitch a tent, go swimming and fishing. Nicholas can take his bike and ride around the paddock when we're tired of the beach.'

Jess grunted. 'Like that's going to happen. It's usually a battle to get him out of the water. A prune is wrinkle-free compared to what he ends up looking like.'

'I've got steak, potatoes wrapped in foil to bake, lots of salad stuff, and fruit for afterwards. How can you refuse?' Jackson implored, looking at her like a little boy intent on winning his case.

'Steak? You don't have any faith in your fishing skills?'

'Fishing? Are we going fishing?' Nicholas leapt between them, looking excited already.

Jackson locked eyes with her. 'Are we? Fishing and camping?'

There wouldn't be any snakes or other creepy-crawlies for her to worry about. 'What are we waiting for?'

Of course, it took nearly an hour to pack clothes, towels, more food, toys and the bike into the truck. Nicholas hindered progress but as he was trying so hard to be helpful Jess didn't growl at him once. His excitement level escalated until it was almost unbearable, and then Jackson stepped in.

'Hey, sport. Take it easy, eh? You need lots of energy to go fishing and swimming, and the way you're going now you'll run out before we leave.'

'Sorry, Jackson. I'll be good, promise.'

Jess shook her head. 'How do you do that?'

'I'm very good at getting my way. With little boys and their wicked mothers. Okay, make that singular. One boy and his mother.' Jackson's hand cupped her butt, squeezed gently. 'Nicholas will go to sleep tonight, won't he?'

Finally she let go of the hurt that had sprung up when Jackson had told her he wouldn't be staying. 'Come on,' she teased him. 'The kid's never been in a tent before. He's going to be wide-eyed all night long.' Chuckling when disappointment darkened Jackson's eyes, she added, 'You can leave behind any condoms you've packed.'

'Which reminds me. Be right back.' He headed outside to the truck. Returning, he handed her a parcel the size of a book.

'What's this?'

'Open it before your young man comes back inside.'

She tore the paper off, became even more baffled at seeing the plain cardboard box. With her fingernail she slit the tape holding down the lid and flicked it open. 'Bleeding heck.' She stared at the condoms. 'You planning on staying around for a while, or just being very busy?'

'That first time? You told me I owed you and I always pay my debts.' Leaning in, he kissed the corner of her mouth. 'Now put them out of sight. I hear small footsteps coming this way. I won't complain if you put a handful in your pocket for later, though.'

'A handful? Yeah, right.' Laughing all the way to her bedroom, she slid the box into the drawer of her bedside table and, yes, shoved some condoms into her overnight bag.

Jess slipped the air-filled bands up Nicholas's arms. 'These'll help keep you afloat in those waves.' Tiny waves that suddenly seemed big compared to her wee boy. 'Hold my hand.'

Small fingers wrapped around hers. 'Will there be fish in the water, Jackson?'

'Not around you. They'll see your legs and swim away fast.' Jackson took his other hand. 'You like swimming, sport?'

'I only like the pool.'

Uh-oh. How did I not know that? Jess bit her lip. 'We'll stay on the edge where it's shallow.' She sank to her knees in the water, the waves reaching the top of her thighs, and reached for Nicholas.

He leaned against her, studying the waves, worry darkening his eyes. 'Why does the sea go up and down like that?'

'Sometimes the wind makes it happen.'

'But there isn't any wind.' Nicholas stared around the small bay.

Jackson squatted down beside them, those well-honed thighs very distracting. 'There might be further away. Or a big boat might've gone past. Engines on boats stir the water like when Mummy makes a cake, and that sends waves inshore.'

'My cakes resemble the sea?'

Jackson grinned and lifted a strand of hair off her face. 'Don't know. You've never made me one.'

'Be grateful.'

Nicholas sank down lower, sucking in his stomach as the water reached his waist. 'It's not cold, Mummy.'

Right. So why the shivers? 'Let's play ball.' Hopefully a game would distract him enough to relax and have fun. She made to take the beach ball from Jackson and came up against hard chest muscles, the hand holding the ball well out of reach. Her gaze shot to his face, caught the cheeky grin. Right, buster. Carefully removing her other hand from Nicholas she turned and shoved at Jackson, toppling him into and under the water.

'Nicholas, help me. Your mother needs controlling.' Jackson coughed out salt water, that grin wider than ever. 'Let's show her she can't play dirty tricks and get away with it.'

Her son didn't need any more encouragement, leaping onto her, wrapping his arms tightly around her knees. Jackson showed no sympathy, helping Nicholas dunk her.

She leapt up, shaking her sodden hair, water streaming down her body. 'Right, who's next?'

'You can't catch me, Mummy.' Nicholas forged through the water, parallel to the shore, shrieking at every splash he made.

Jackson took her hand and they pretended to chase

him hard, keeping close enough to reach him quickly if needed but letting him think he was winning. Inevitably he tripped himself up and went under. Jess felt the air stall in her lungs. He'd panic and choke.

Jackson lunged forward, caught Nicholas and stood him on his feet. 'You okay, sport?'

Wide-eyed and grinning, Nicholas shouted, 'Yes. Look at me, Mummy.' He jumped up, tucking his knees under his chin and dropped into the water again.

'Guess he likes the sea as much as the pool, then.' She was relieved. Living in Golden Bay meant he'd spend a lot of time on or near the water and if he feared it then he wouldn't learn to master it.

'What happened to that ball?' Jackson looked around. 'Oops, it's heading out. I'd better retrieve it before it gets too far away.' He dived in and swam for it, his strokes strong and powerful, pulling his body quickly through the water.

'Mummy, I want to swim like Jackson.'

Thank you, Jackson. Until now, learning to swim had been the last thing Nicholas had wanted to do. The pool had been about splashing and jumping. She ruffled his wet hair. 'I'll sign you up for lessons this week.' And thank Jackson in an appropriate fashion once her boy was asleep.

'Help me collect driftwood for a bonfire, Nicholas.' Jackson threw an armful of wood down on the damp sand. The tide was receding fast and they'd be able to light a small fire before darkness set in.

'Why are we having a fire?' the boy asked.

'So we can toast marshmallows on sticks and eat them after dinner.'

'Won't they melt?'

Sometimes Nicholas was smarter than he should be for his age. 'Not if you're quick.'

'Are we all sleeping in the tent?' Nicholas picked up the end of a huge piece of wood and staggered along the beach, dragging it behind him.

'Yes.' Damn it. He hadn't thought that far ahead when he'd had this camping brainwave. Hadn't considered the frustration of lying with Jess and not being able to make love to her because Nicholas would be with them. It had seemed like a brilliant idea to come out here and give the boy a new experience. Guess he'd have to rein in his hormones for the night. Unless they found a secluded spot away from the tent but close enough to hear if Nicholas woke and got frightened.

'Hey, you two,' Jess called from down by the water's edge. 'Come and help me collect some cockles to cook for dinner.'

'What are cockles?'

'Shellfish,' Jackson told him. 'They're yummy.' If you got rid of all the sand in the shells.

'Why don't we catch them with our rods?'

'Because they live in the sand and mud. You've got to dig for them. See, like Mummy's doing.' Jess looked stunning in that orange bikini she wore. All legs and breasts. His mouth dried. When she'd asked if he intended staying on at Golden Bay he'd struggled to say no. Which meant he should be hightailing it out of the country now, not planning a way to get into her sleeping bag tonight.

There was no denying Jess had sneaked in under his skin when he'd been busy looking the other way. Leaving her was going to be incredibly difficult. But he couldn't take her and Nicholas with him. His eighteenth-floor apartment was definitely not conducive to raising a young child. No, Nicholas was in the perfect place for a boy—

swimming and fishing on his doorstep, farms with real animals just as close in the other direction.

'I want to do the digging, Mummy.' Once Nicholas got started there was no stopping him. Finally they had to drag him into the water and clean off the mud that covered him from head to toes. 'Why are you throwing them away?' he asked when Jackson tipped half their haul back into the mud.

'Because we're not allowed too many.'

'Will the policeman tell us off if you don't put them back?'

'Yes. It's so that we don't use them all up and can get more another day.'

'Okay.'

Okay. Life seemed so simple for Nicholas. Give him an explanation and he was happy, not looking for hidden agendas. 'How about you and I cook the cockles so that Mummy can have a rest?' Jess's all-night haul at the birthing unit appeared to be catching up with her. He'd seen her hiding a yawn more than once. 'Jess, why don't you curl up in the tent and have a snooze?'

'Because I'd probably not wake up till morning. I don't want to miss out on anything.' Her smile was soft and wistful.

'I promise to call you for dinner.' He knew what all-nighters with patients were like. They drained you so that putting one foot in front of the other became hard work. 'Go on. Nicholas and I will put our rods in the water and see what we can catch. On your way to the tent can you put those cockles in fresh water so they spit out the sand?' He wasn't giving her a chance to argue.

'You promise to call me?'

'Promise. I'll have a glass of wine waiting. The potatoes will be cooking and the steak ready to sizzle.'

Another yawn stretched her mouth and she shrugged. 'Guess I can't argue with that.' Picking up the bucket of shellfish, she trudged up the beach and across the road to their camp site.

Jackson only tore his eyes away from her when she reached the tent. His heart ached with need. With love. Love? No way, man. He hadn't gone and fallen in love with Jessica. No way. So why the pain in his chest? Why the need to wrap her up and look after her? Why spend time with her little boy, teaching him things any father would do if he wasn't in love with Jess?

No, he couldn't be. It wasn't meant to happen like that. Lots of hot sex, and plenty of fun; that was how it went. Harmless, enjoyable, no ties, no future.

He dropped to his haunches and picked up a pebble to hurl it across the water. Where had he gone wrong? How had he made such a monumental error? Right from that first night he'd had no intention of getting too close to Jess. Because no matter what happened, what she hoped for, he was going home to Hong Kong. To his frantic life, his orderly life. His now frightening life—and that damned promise.

Another pebble skimmed across the wavelets. Dropped out of sight under the water. And another, and another. A lonely life it may be, but at least he wasn't letting anyone down by being too busy for them.

What about Ping's words of wisdom last week when he'd finally caught up with him on the phone? *You are ready to return home. Hong Kong isn't home for you.* Ping had sounded so certain that he'd found he couldn't argue with his friend. Not that he'd done anything stupid like hand in his notice. No way. But he hadn't been able to shut Ping out of his brain, especially in the early hours while he lay in bed, waiting for the sun to lift above the horizon so he could go for a run. Ping often came out with Chinese proverbs or other wise bits of advice, but this time Jackson would ignore him.

He might be falling for Jess but he wouldn't be doing anything about it. He wasn't prepared to live in the back of beyond where his medical skills would be wasted. And he couldn't ask Jess to move when she'd only recently settled here and begun making a secure environment for Nicholas to grow up in.

'Look at me. I can throw stones in the water like you.' Nicholas stood beside him, his little face earnest as he tried to toss his pebbles as far as the water's edge.

Might be time to head away, get out of here earlier than planned, save any further heartache that being with Jess would cause. Then there was this little guy who took everything at face value and had accepted him as a part of his life.

'You're doing great, Nicholas.' Jackson stood up and moved behind him, took his elbow and gently pulled it back. 'Swing your arm back like this. Now fling it forward as hard as you can.'

They continued throwing pebbles until Nicholas tired of that game. 'Can we go fishing now?'

'Sure. I'll go and get the rods and bait.'

'I'll do it.' Without waiting for Jackson, Nicholas raced up the beach. 'I know where the rods are.' He was nearing the road too fast.

'Nicholas, come back here now.' Panic had Jackson charging after him. 'Don't you go on that road, Nicholas,' he roared. He thought he could hear a vehicle approaching at speed. 'Nicholas. Stop.'

'I'm looking both ways.'

'Wait for me.' Jackson skidded to a stop beside him at the road's edge. His hand gripped the boy's shoulder.

'Never run towards a road, sport,' he gasped around his receding fear. 'Cars go a lot faster than you do and the driver might not see you.'

'Mummy told me that.' Nicholas wriggled his shoulder free and looked right, left, then right again. 'See. Nothing's coming. Can I cross now?'

That vehicle had to have been in his imagination because now he'd stopped his mad dash up the beach Jackson couldn't hear it. Quickly checking both ways, he said in an uneven voice, 'Yes, you can. Let's go quietly so we don't wake your mum.'

Over an hour later Jackson and Nicholas returned from their fishing expedition with all the bait gone and no fish to show for it.

'I wanted to catch a fish.' Nicholas pouted. 'It's not fair.'

'That's the way of it, sport. If fish were too easy to catch, there'd be no fun in it.' Jackson stopped at the tent entrance and peered in. Jess lay sprawled face down across the bigger of the two air beds, her hair spread over the pillow. How easy it would be to curl up beside her and push his fingers through that blonde silk. Fishy fingers, he reminded himself.

He turned to Nicholas. 'Let's go clean ourselves up. Then we'll get dinner cooking and wake your mother.'

'I'm hungry now.'

'Wash your hands first. You smell of fish bait.'

'I want something to eat first.'

Jackson sighed. No wonder Jess gave in to Nicholas so often. Otherwise she'd be sounding like the big, bad wolf all the time. 'You can have a banana as soon as you're clean.' He swung Nicholas up under his arm and carried him to the ablutions block, tickling him and getting ear-piercing shrieks for his efforts. So much for keeping quiet, but at least the temper tantrum had been avoided.

With the potatoes baking on the barbecue hot plate and the cockles in a pot ready to steam, Jackson poured a glass of wine and headed for the tent. 'Wake up, sleepy-head.' His heart blocked his throat at the sight inside. Jess had rolled onto her back and spread her arms wide, like an invitation. In sleep she had lost that worrying look that had him wondering if she'd got too involved with him, making it easier for him to believe they were merely having an affair that he would shortly walk away from unharmed. Except he already knew it would hurt, that he was too late to save his heart. But he would still have to go.

'Jess.' He nudged her foot with his toe. 'Time to wake up, lazybones.'

'Go away,' she mumbled, and made to roll over.

'Mummy, you've got to get up now.' Nicholas bounced onto the bed and dropped to his knees so close to Jess that Jackson feared she'd be bruised.

Her eyes popped open. 'Hello, you two.' Her voice was thick with sleep. Rubbing her hands down her cheeks, she yawned and then stretched her feet to the end of the bed and her hands high above her, lifting her breasts as she did.

His breath caught as he ogled those sweet mounds pushing against her singlet top. The glass shook in his hand, spilling wine over his fingers. 'I'll see you outside. Do you want this wine in here?'

'No, I'll join you in a minute.' Already she was scrambling onto her knees and delving into her bag to haul out a jersey.

Nicholas had arranged the outdoor chairs so that they could see down the grass to the beach. Jackson sank down on one and picked up his beer. His hand still shook. He knew how it felt to hold Jess in his arms and make love to her, the little sounds she made in pleasure, the way she liked to wind her legs around his afterwards. He wanted to know all those things again and again.

Making love to Jess was nothing like the sex he'd had with those women he usually dated. But he hadn't really dated Jess. They'd just got together. At work, at his parents' place, and mostly at her home, where they enjoyed each other whenever Nicholas wasn't around or was tucked up in bed, sound asleep.

'Where's the TV?' Nicholas asked as he crossed over to Jackson.

Laughter rang out, sweet and clear, from the tent. 'There's no TV out here, sweetheart. When you go camping you don't have power for things like that.'

As the boy's face began to pucker up Jackson reined in his smile and said, 'Think about telling your friends how you spent the night in a tent and that you ate food cooked outside, and how you dug for shellfish. Isn't that more exciting?'

'Can I catch a fish tomorrow?'

'We'll give it a darned good try, sport.'

Jess slid onto the chair beside him, her light jersey covering those tantalising breasts. 'You have a knack with him.' She sipped from her glass. 'Perfect.'

'Should've got champagne, knowing how much you enjoy it.'

'You'd better stop spoiling me. I might get used to it.' She stared out across the water, seeing who knew what. The glass shook in her fingers, as it had moments ago in his.

Laying a hand on her thigh, he squeezed gently. 'Jess, I can't—'

She turned, placed a finger on his lips. 'Don't say anything, Jackson. I know this has to come to an end, have known it all along, but I don't want to spoil our time together talking about things we can't change.'

He could not argue with that, so he didn't.

CHAPTER EIGHT

'So MELANIE'S GETTING a little sister or brother. That's cool.' *And I'm fighting something very like jealousy here.* Jess watched Sasha's face light up with excitement, felt her own heart thump harder. *A baby—with Jackson— would be perfect.* She breathed in deep, exhaled slowly. *Get real.*

'Yeah, isn't it? I can't wait. So unlike last time, when I was dealing with the defection of Melanie's father and coming to terms with returning here, this time I've got Grady right beside me.' Sasha grinned and wrapped her arms around Jess in a big hug. 'Know a good midwife?'

'I might.' She squeezed back. 'A summer baby.'

'Not like Melanie. She kept me warm through last winter.' Sasha stepped away and opened the fridge, where she found the salmon Jackson had placed there earlier. 'Did Jackson go out to Anatoki for this?'

Anatoki was a salmon farm where customers could fish for their dinner in large holding ponds. 'He took Nicholas and let him catch the salmon. In fact, Jackson let him catch and release two before bringing this one home. I don't think my boy will ever stop talking about that. I'm surprised he hasn't told you every minute detail. I couldn't get his fishing shirt off him so he does reek a little.'

Sasha shook her head. 'I haven't spoken to him yet. He's following Jackson everywhere, glued to his hip.'

'There's a certain amount of hero worship going on, for sure.' Which would soon turn into a big problem. The weeks were speeding by and when Jackson headed away she'd be left to pick up the pieces. As well as deal with her own broken heart.

Sasha looked up from stuffing the salmon with herbs. 'You're worried?'

'Big time. Maybe I should've stopped seeing Jackson right after your wedding and kept him out of Nicholas's life.' Like she'd have been able to manage that easily. She'd fallen for him so fast she'd been spinning.

'Maybe you should tell Jackson how you feel about him.' Sasha cocked her head to one side. 'Hmm?'

'No way. We've been up front right from the start. No commitment, no demands on each other. Have a good time and sign off come April.' Why did that sound so flippant? Because it was. Casual maybe, but not normal. 'But I haven't, and won't, tell him I've fallen for him. It would ruin everything.'

Her friend's lips pressed tight for a moment and Jess knew she was about to get a lecture. 'Leave it, Sasha. I'm not asking Jackson to stay on when he obviously doesn't want to. Don't forget I'm not interested in tying myself to anyone either. It wouldn't be fair on Nicholas.'

'That's getting a little monotonous, Jess. You've got a big heart, big enough for more than your son. You've spread it around the community and he hasn't suffered.' Hadn't she already heard that from Jackson? Unfortunately, Sasha wasn't finished. 'There are still a few weeks for you to talk to him, lay your feelings on the line.'

Jess shivered. She couldn't do that. Too scary. 'Do we want to make the salads now?'

Sasha wasn't about to be sidetracked. 'Think about it. What have you got to lose? A broken heart? That's coming anyway, regardless. But you might find my brother has changed his mind about his mighty Hong Kong hospital and lifestyle. He was moody when he first arrived home, got angry at the smallest things, but that's not happening so much now. Mum says he sometimes sings in the shower. That's unheard of. You've got a role in all this. He's keen on you, really keen.'

Jackson hadn't told his family about the stabbing. He didn't want them worrying about him when he returned to Hong Kong. Opening the fridge again, Jess removed the vegetable bin containing everything needed to put together a crisp, healthy salad. Jackson might be keen on her, as Sasha put it, but he didn't want her trailing after him all the way to Asia. That also would mean putting her needs before Nicholas's. How could she explain to her boy that living in an enormous city was as good as being in Golden Bay with beaches and fishing?

Loud laughter rolled through the open windows. Jackson and Grady were playing soccer with Nicholas on the front lawn. Her son wore a huge grin as he charged after the ball and stole it from under Jackson's foot. He dribbled it towards the makeshift goal until he fell over the ball and landed on his face. Jess held her breath, waiting for an explosion of tears, but Nicholas bounced back up and took off after the ball that Grady had stolen while he was down. Her boy was lapping up the male attention. 'Grady will still have some time for Nicholas, won't he?'

'You know he will, though it won't be the same as having Jackson's undivided attention.' Sasha handed her a glass of champagne. 'You'll have to drink my share now that I'm pregnant. Let's join Mum and Dad on the deck. The salmon will take a while.'

Jess continued to keep one eye on Jackson, filing away memories of how athletic he looked, how his long legs ate up the ground as he chased the ball, how his laughter sneaked under her ribs and tickled her heart. She collected even more mental images during dinnertime.

But. Nothing was going to be the same ever again. Grady might be there for Nicholas when he had time, but he had his own children to put first. She'd do anything to make her son's life perfect—except tell Jackson she loved him.

But as Sasha had pointed out, what did she have to lose? Honesty was good, wasn't it? What if Jackson had already guessed her feelings for him? Was he waiting for her to say something? Or crossing his fingers she'd keep silent?

'You're very quiet tonight.' Jackson leaned close.

Unnerved that he might read her mind, she shivered. 'Sorry.'

'You're cold. I'll get your jersey.'

She let him go and find it. Cold had nothing to do with that shiver. But—but all to do with cowardice. She was afraid if she told Jackson she loved him he'd laugh at her or, worse, commiserate and beat a hasty retreat. So she'd remain silent. Coward. If her heart was big enough for more than Nicholas, as people kept telling her, then what was holding her back? Nothing ventured, nothing gained, as they said. Or nothing lost.

But. She was hanging onto her belief that she'd turn out to be like her parents. Did Sasha have a point? Was this belief just an excuse to hide behind because she was afraid of putting her heart on the line? It had hurt when Nicholas's father had done a bunk, and now, compared with her feelings for Jackson, she saw she hadn't been as invested in that relationship as she'd thought.

'Here.' Jackson held out her jersey. 'Have you taken to buying everything you wear in orange since the wedding?' Those delicious lips curved upwards, sending her stomach into a riot of fluttering.

'No, but I have bought things in apricot shades.' Underwear, two shirts and the sexiest pair of fitted jeans. 'Online shopping is an absolute boon when living here.'

Jackson did an eye-roll. 'Women will always find a way to shop, even if they're living on Mars.'

'Sexist.' Jess and Sasha spoke in unison.

Virginia added her bit. 'So says the man with the biggest, most expensive wardrobe I've ever seen.'

'Nicholas. Want another game of soccer, sport?' Jackson grinned.

'After dinner. I want to eat more salmon. It's yummy, Mummy. Can you take me to catch more?'

Giving Jackson a mock glare, she answered, 'You've been spoiled today. This is a treat.'

'We'll go next time I come home, sport.'

She'd have sworn she was trying not to look at him, but she was—staring. 'You might come home for another visit?' she croaked in a squeaky voice that had everyone staring at them both. Don't. It won't be fair on Nicholas. Or me.

'We'd love it if you do.' Ian filled the sudden silence. 'But we understand how busy you are over there.'

Jackson looked embarrassed, like he'd made a mistake. 'I've got more leave owing but it's hard to get away. There's always a shortage of temporary replacement staff.' Backpedalling so fast he'd fall on his butt if he wasn't careful.

Jess forced her disappointment aside. What had she expected? Glancing around the now quiet table, she saw that Jackson's statement had taken a toll on everyone. Of course Ian and Virginia wanted their son staying home. Now that Virginia was ill it would be more important for them. Sasha would want her brother on hand to help out on the orchard and to be a part of her children's lives. Everyone was affected by Jackson's decision and yet he should be able to continue with the career path he'd chosen.

Her gaze stopped on Jackson, noted the way his jaw clenched, his lips whitened. This was the first time he'd got angry in a couple of weeks. Was he angry at himself for hurting his family? Reaching under the table, she laid a hand on his thigh and softly dug her fingers into those tense muscles. 'Do they make apricot-coloured fishing rods?'

Green eyes locked with hers. Recognition of how she was trying to help him flickered back at her. His Adam's apple bobbed. Then his mouth softened. 'No, but I'm sure I can find you an orange one.'

The chuckles around the table were a little forced but soon the conversation was flowing again, this time on safer topics.

Not all the questions buzzing around inside Jess's head retreated. Instead, they drove her loopy with apprehension, making her feel like she was on a runaway truck, with no hope of stopping, and only disaster at the end. When Jackson offered to drive her home, she shook her head. 'Not tonight. My boy's exhausted and so am I. An early night is what we need.' She needed space to cope with the growing fear of how she'd manage when he left.

'You're mad at me for saying earlier I'd go fishing with Nicholas again some time.' He stood directly in front of her, hands on hips, eyes locked on hers.

'Not mad, Jackson, disappointed. Nicholas is young.

He only sees things in black and white, and everything happens now.' That was only the beginning of her turmoil.

'Yeah, I get it. I'm very sorry. I'm not used to youngsters and how their thought processes work.'

'Says the man who has been absolutely brilliant with Nicholas these past two months.' She dug her keys out of her bag. 'Just so you know, I'm not going home alone because of what you told him. I'm bigger than that. I really do need some sleep.' Some space in my bed so I can think, and not be distracted by your sexy body and persuasive voice.

His lips brushed her cheek. 'I get that, too. I think. Let me put Nicholas in his car seat.'

She watched with hunger as he strode into the lounge where Nicholas was watching TV with Ian. She watched when he came back with her boy tucked against his chest, Nicholas's thumb in his mouth as he desperately tried to stay awake. Her hunger increased as he carefully clicked the seat belt around her son and brushed curls off his face. She shouldn't have turned him down. Climbing inside her car, she watched as he bent down and kissed her, long and tenderly. So tenderly he brought tears to her eyes. And a lump to her throat. She needed to be with him. She needed to be alone.

Jackson watched Jess drive out onto the road for the short trip back to her place. It took all his willpower not to run after her, to follow her home and slip into bed to hold her tight.

How the hell was he going to leave Jess? His heart ached now and he still had four weeks left to be with her. Impossible to imagine how he'd feel once he stepped onto that plane heading northeast.

Don't go. Stay here. Everyone wants you to. That much

had been painfully obvious at dinnertime. Surprising how easy it might be to do exactly that. Stay. Become a part of the community he'd been in such a hurry to leave when he'd been a teen. If he stayed, what would he do for work? On average he'd have one emergency a week to deal with. Unless he worked in Nelson. Only two hours' drive away. He could commute or get a small apartment, return home on his days off. Not the perfect way to have a relationship but it had worked for Mum and Dad. Nah, he did not want that for him and Jess.

As the taillights of Jess's car disappeared he headed for the deck and some quiet time. Inside, Sasha and Mum were arguing light-heartedly about who had the best chocolate-cake recipe. Dad was still watching TV. Or was he catnapping, as he often did when he thought no one was looking?

Family. He loved them. Leaving Golden Bay back then hadn't been about them. Being young and brash, he'd always believed they would be around for ever. That whenever he chose to return, family life would be as it had always been. And it was. Yet it was different. There were additions: Grady, Melanie and the unborn baby. Dad no longer disappeared to the other side of the world every second week. Then there was Mum. His rock when he'd been growing up, always there with a ready ear and a loving word. Now he should be here for her. That promise shouldn't keep him from those he loved, yet he was afraid to ignore it. His word was important.

He was avoiding the real issue. Jessica Baxter.

Jess hadn't had what he and Sasha got from Mum and Dad, yet she'd slotted into his family: best mates with Sasha; a surrogate daughter to his parents. Often she could be found helping out in the orchard or doing the ironing or scrubbing the floor. If anyone was the outsider in his family it was him. Only because he lived so damned far away, but it was reason enough.

'Want a beer?' Grady's question cut through the crap in his head.

'Thanks.' He took the proffered bottle, dropped onto a chair and swung his feet up onto the deck railing. The cold liquid was like nectar. 'That's bloody good.'

'Nothing's ever easy, is it?'

He presumed Grady was talking about the things going on in his head. 'Nope.'

They sat in a comfortable silence, drinking their beer, replenishing the bottles when they dried up, not bothering with unnecessary talk. They both knew the situation. Why keep talking about it? As far as brothers-in-law went, Sasha had got him a good one.

The temperature had cooled, and the air felt heavy with dew. Summer was giving way to autumn and the temperatures were beginning to reflect that, day and night. Soon the holiday homeowners would clean down their boats and put them away for winter. They'd lock up their houses and go home. What would Jess do over winter? Would she hunker down for the cold months or get out there, continuing to visit people: checking they had enough firewood to see them through; taking food and books to the older folk living outside the township boundaries; keeping an eye on their health?

No guesses there. He knew the answer. Jess was generous beyond generous. No matter that she thought it was about repaying folk for the bad things she'd done as a wild teenager. It wasn't that at all. Jess was kind and generous to a fault. Couldn't help being so good to others.

'Time we went home, Grady.' Sasha stepped into the light spilling from the windows. 'Melanie has finished feeding and needs to be tucked up in her cot.'

'Not a problem, sweetheart.' Grady unwound his long body and stood up. 'You want to do a spot of fishing tomorrow, Jackson? We could put the tinny in before breakfast and go find ourselves something for brunch.'

'I'm on. See you about six?' Fishing always relaxed him. Unless he was with Nicholas and had to spend the whole time baiting hooks and untying knots in the line. Which was kind of fun, in its own way.

'Six? Just because you're sleeping solo tonight, you want to drag me out early.'

'Five past?' Jackson laughed, but inside he felt lonely. Grady was a good bloke, but he wasn't what he needed right now, at night, in bed. No, she had elected to go home alone.

Jess might've desperately wanted to sleep, but that didn't mean she got any. At two o'clock she gave up and went out to the kitchen to make some chamomile tea. Sitting in the lounge, she switched on the TV and watched the second half of some out-of-date rerun of something she'd first seen when she'd been about fourteen. And still the thoughts about what she should tell Jackson before he left went round and round her skull.

'Hey, Jackson, I love you. So if you ever change your mind about coming home or wanting a life partner, you know my number.'

Yep, that would work. She could see him rushing up and kissing her and telling her that was the best news he'd had in a long time. Not.

Okay, what about, 'Jackson, I love you and would love it if Nicholas and I could move to Hong Kong to be with you.'

He probably wouldn't bother packing his bags, just run for the airport.

What about just shutting up, keeping her feelings to herself, and getting on with enjoying the remaining weeks?

Yep, that might work.

Except she'd heard Sasha loud and clear. It was time to risk her heart, lay it out there for Jackson to do with as he pleased. At least she'd know exactly where she stood with him.

Thought I knew that already.

They were having an affair; no more, no less. She'd fallen in love with him the night it had started but she'd known from the beginning that the fling had no chance of becoming anything else. It'd be breaking the rules to tell Jackson her true feelings.

Rules were made to be broken, weren't they?

Apparently, but…she drew a deep breath…this could backfire so fast, so badly, she daren't do it.

She had to do it. It was eating her up, not being honest with him.

Why had she fallen for him? Why Jackson, of all men? Because he was out of reach and so she'd be safe? Wouldn't have to relinquish her long-held beliefs that she couldn't love more than one person thoroughly?

Newsflash. You already do love Nicholas and Jackson, and you haven't once let your boy down in the weeks you've been seeing Jackson. You are so not like your parents it's a joke.

The annoying voice in her head hadn't finished with her yet. 'You love Jackson because he's Jackson, because of all the little things that make him the man he is. The good things and the not-so-good things.' Huh? 'The immaculate clothes that are so out of place here, the need to be in charge.' Oh. 'Remember the colour of love is sky blue. Happy blue with bright yellow sunshine.'

CHAPTER NINE

THE COLOUR OF love was absent the next morning as Jess drove to the Wilson household. The sky was grey with heavy, rain-filled clouds and they were going nowhere. The moist atmosphere felt chilly after such a hot summer.

Her heart was out of whack, like it didn't know what rhythm it should be beating. It sure clogged her throat any time she thought about her mission.

'So don't think about it.' Yeah, sure.

'What can't I think about, Mummy?'

'Sorry, sweetheart. I was talking to myself.' Turning into the long driveway leading up to Ian and Virginia's house, her foot lifted off the accelerator and the car slowly came to a halt. *What am I doing? Is it the right thing?* The resolve she'd found at about six that morning had deserted her. *Turn around and go home. No. That's cowardly.*

Before she could overthink what she'd come to do, she pressed her foot hard on the accelerator and the car shot up the drive like she was being chased.

'Hi, Jess, Nicholas. You're out early.' Ian sauntered over to them from his packing shed. 'Just like the boys. Grady was around here before the sparrows woke to take Jackson out fishing.'

Her heart stopped its erratic tattoo as relief whooshed

through her. *Coward. This is a delay, not the finish of your mission.* 'Isn't it a bit rough out on the water today?'

Ian shook his head. 'No. Flat calm at the moment. Perfect conditions. Though it is forecast to kick up early afternoon, but they'll be back long before then. Hopefully with a bin of fish for lunch.'

'Fishing? I want to go, too.'

'No, Nicholas, you can't.' Thump-thump went the dull pain behind her eyes. The last thing she needed was Nicholas throwing a paddy because he hadn't gone with Jackson. Picking him up, she hugged him tight. 'Sorry, sweetheart.'

Ian ruffled Nicholas's hair. 'Sorry, boyo, but Grady and Jackson were having some man time. None of us were invited.'

'What's man time?' came the inevitable question.

Jess held her breath as Ian answered, keen to know what this fishing trip was all about if not catching fish.

'It's when close friends want to spend time talking or not talking and doing something together that they enjoy.'

What did Jackson and Grady have to talk about that they hadn't already discussed last night around the dinner table?

'Guess we'll go back home, then.' She sighed. Home, where she could pace up and down the small lounge. Or make herself useful and bake cookies for her neighbours. Or, 'Think I'll go see Sasha.'

Ian frowned. 'Don't go before you've seen Virginia, will you? She's a bit shaky this morning and I don't mind admitting she worries me. I never know how she's really feeling, she's so intent on hiding the truth from me.'

Guilt assailed her. She'd become very selfish recently, putting her own concerns before those of her friends. See, loving Jackson did divert her from the other people in her life. 'Of course I'm going to see Virginia. Is there something you want me to check out?'

'No. There are two doctors in the family taking good care of her. Driving her insane with all their questions if you want to know the truth. But while I can sympathise with Virginia, I need those boys doing the doctor thing.' Ian looked glum as he ran a hand through his hair. Like father, like son. 'Just give her some cheek and pretend everything's normal, will you?'

'Come on, Nicholas. Let's go say hello to Virginia.'

'He can help me in the shed, if you like.' Ian looked at Nicholas. 'We've got boxes to make up for the avocados.'

'Yes, please. I want to help.'

'Guess that's decided, then.' Jess headed for the house, torn between being relieved Jackson wasn't around to talk to and being disappointed she hadn't got it over and done with.

Jackson wound hard and fast, bringing the line in before the barracuda bit into the blue cod he'd hooked. 'Get lost, you waste of sea space.'

'You've got two cod on those hooks.' Grady grinned. 'Talk about greedy.'

'Saves time.' Jackson swung the straining line over the side of the boat so that his catch landed in the big bin they'd put on board. 'Nothing wrong with either of them either. Definitely not undersized.' He grinned. Not like Grady's last two.

'Next you'll be saying you've caught the biggest of the day.'

'Too right.' One of the cod had swallowed the hook, making it tricky to remove. He found the special pliers and wrenched it free. The other fish was foul-hooked around the mouth and didn't take much to undo. 'Got my brunch. How're you doing?'

'I'm onto getting enough for the rest of the family.' Grady wound in a fish and Jackson nearly split his sides laughing.

'Not even Nicholas would get enough to eat from that.'

'Says the expert,' Grady grumped, and carefully slid the undersized cod back under the water. 'You and that boy get on okay.'

'He likes fishing.' Hopefully Grady would take him out occasionally. 'I'll miss him.'

'What about his mother? Going to miss her, too?'

'Definitely.' More than he'd have believed possible. Hell, he missed her now, missed her whenever they were apart. It had hurt last night when she'd wanted to go home alone. But she was entitled to her space. He didn't want to encroach on everything she did. Not much, anyway.

'There's a job going at the Nelson Hospital ED.'

That he did not want to know. It added to his dilemma about heading away, leaving everyone behind. 'I've got one, thanks.'

Grady dropped his line back in the water. 'Just thought you should know.'

A tug at the end of his line gave Jackson the distraction he needed. Winding fast, he soon had another cod in the bin. 'One to go and we've got our limit.'

And we can head home to the family. My family. And Jess and Nicholas.

Jess placed the tray of shortbread in the oven and set the timer. It was quiet in her house. Nicholas had stayed on with Ian, doing man stuff apparently. Thank goodness there were men like Ian to give her boy a male perspective. Jackson was Nicholas's firm favourite. Unfortunately. His little heart would be broken soon. Had she done wrong, encouraging Nicholas to get on with Jackson? Probably. But, then, life was like that and the sooner Nicholas learned he had to look out for himself the better.

Her cellphone vibrated on the bench. 'Hello?'

'I think I'm in labour.'

'Constance? Is that you?' The thirty-six-year-old woman wasn't due for ten days.

'Yes.' Grunt. 'Can you hurry? You know how fast my babies like to be.'

'On my way.' Turning the oven off, she ran for her car, whilst phoning Virginia. 'I've got an eminent birth. Can Nicholas stay there until I'm finished?' She hated asking when Virginia had enough to deal with, but right now she didn't have the time to collect her boy and deposit him with Andrea and Bobby. 'I can phone Andrea and see if she'll pick him up later.'

'Nonsense. We love having him here. Don't worry about him at all. Just go and deliver that baby safely.'

Nicholas waved furiously as they turned up the drive. Jackson looked around, felt a tug of disappointment when he didn't see Jess's car. 'Hey, sport. What have you been up to all morning?'

'Making boxes. Did you get any fish?' Nicholas jumped up and down by the boat, trying to get high enough to see what they'd caught.

Jackson swung him up and into the boat. 'Take a look in that bin.'

Nicholas's eyes popped out wide. 'That's lots. They're very big.' He delved into the bin, ran his hands all over the cold, wet fish. Jess would be thrilled when she caught up with her stinky boy.

'Where's Mummy?' The question was out before he'd thought about it.

Grady rolled his eyes and hefted the bin out of the boat.

'She's getting a new baby.' Nicholas picked up a rod and handed it to him.

Grady's eyes widened and his mouth twitched. 'Interesting.'

'Careful of those hooks, sport.' Jackson took the rod and stood it against the side of the boat and waited for the second rod to come his way. Jess was at a birth. He remembered when Baby Carter had been born and the misty look of longing that had filtered into her eyes. Did she really want more children? Or did she get like that with every birth she attended?

'You're looking dewy-eyed.' Grady nudged him.

Jackson snapped his head around. 'What? I don't think so. I am definitely not interested in babies. Not when I've got to go back to Hong Kong anyway. No, sir.'

'The man protests too much. Come on, Nicholas. Help me clean up these fish.' Grady strolled off to the outside sink and table to fillet the fish, Nicholas stepping along beside him.

Do I want children? Now? With Jess? Turning the hose on, he began hosing down the boat and trailer to remove any traces of salt water.

Yes. Someday. Yes. Cold water sprayed down his trousers, filled his shoes. Damn. Concentrate on the job in hand. Stop asking himself stupid questions. Whatever he wanted, it wasn't going to happen.

So whose baby was Jess delivering?

'Abigail is absolutely beautiful.' As Jess handed Constance her daughter she heard a vehicle pulling up outside the house. 'You've got a visitor, Tim.'

Tim groaned. 'Bad timing.' He didn't move from

where he sat on the edge of the bed his wife had just given birth in.

'Want me to go give whoever it is a nudge?' Jess figured these two needed time alone with Abigail and it was an excuse to take herself out of the room.

'Would you mind?' Tim looked hopeful. 'Though I guess if it's one of our parents there's no stopping them.'

'Leave it to me.' She was already halfway out of the room. The doorbell chimed before she reached the front of the house. Pulling the door wide, the breath stuck in her lungs.

Jackson stood there, beaming at her. 'Thought I'd drop by and see if you needed any support.'

Leaning against the doorjamb for strength, she waited for her breathing to restart. 'You're too late. Abigail arrived ten minutes ago.'

His brow creased. 'That was fast. From what Mum said, you've only been gone a little over an hour.'

'Constance has a history of short labours, hence the home birth. She didn't fancy giving birth in Tim's truck on the way to town.'

Nodding, Jackson said, 'So you're all done here? Heading back to town now?'

'I've got some cleaning up to do, and I like to hang around for a while in case there's anything not right. Though Constance is a seasoned mum, this being her fourth baby.' But she wasn't about to leave because of that. 'I'm about to make coffee. Want one?' Hopefully the caffeine wouldn't set her heart racing any faster than it already was. One sight of Jackson and it lost all control over its rhythm.

'Sounds good.'

Pushing away from the jamb, she straightened. 'How was the fishing?'

'Brilliant. You've got blue cod for dinner.' He caught her elbow, held her from moving away. 'Did you get any of that sleep you wanted? You're looking more peaky than ever.'

'Flattery will get you anything.' She tugged free, only to be caught again.

'What's bothering you, Jess?' Those green eyes bored into her, seeing who knew what? Probably everything she was trying to hide from him.

So stop hiding it. Get it over and done. Stepping past him, she tugged the door shut and went down the steps to the path. Rotating on her heels, she faced him, locked eyes with him again. 'You. Me. Us. That's what's keeping me awake at the moment.'

He froze, stared at her like he was a deer caught in headlights. His Adam's apple bobbed. The tip of his tongue slid across his bottom lip. Fear tripped through that green gaze. 'Us.'

Nodding slowly, she added, 'I know we agreed to an affair for the duration of your time here.' Damn, that sounded too formal, but how else did she say what needed to be said? *Try coming straight out with it.* 'But I fell in love with you.'

His face paled. Not a good sign. At all. Might as well give him the rest. Might help put him at ease. 'You're safe. I said at the time I had no intention of ever getting into a permanent relationship with anyone. That hasn't changed.' *You are so wrong, Jess. You'd settle down with Jackson in a flash, given the opportunity.* Yes, now she understood she would. No argument.

The next thing she knew his arms were around her, holding her tight against his chest. Under her ear his heart was speeding faster than a rabbit being chased by hounds. 'I'm so sorry, Jess.'

'I think that should be my line,' she muttered. But why? What had she done wrong? It wasn't as though she'd been able to avoid falling for him. It had happened in an instant. Yet she repeated in a lower voice, 'I'm sorry.'

'Ahh, Jess, this is all my fault. I've been so selfish. But I couldn't stay away from you.' Still holding her around the waist, he leaned back to lock eyes with her. 'You are beautiful, inside and out, Jessica Baxter. I've never known anyone like you.'

'Yet you're still going away.' Wanting to pull away before she melded herself to him so he had to take her with him, but needing to stay in his arms for as long as she could, she stood irresolute, fighting threatening tears.

'I'm sorry.' His voice was low, and sad, and trembling. 'Very sorry for everything.'

Jess spun out of his arms and tore down the path out onto the roadside, gulping lungful after lungful of air as she went. Get a grip. She'd known this would hurt big time. Yeah, but knowing and experiencing were poles apart. This hurt so bad she felt like she might never be able to stand straight again. She loved Jackson. End of story. There'd be no happy ever after. Funny how now that she knew that for real, she realised how much she actually wanted it. Desperately.

'Jess.' Jackson had followed her, stood watching her through wary eyes. 'Are you all right?'

'Oh, I'm just peachy.' She gasped, tried to hold onto the words bursting from her throat, and failed. 'Of course I'm not all right. I've spent days agonising over whether to tell you or not, but honesty got the better of me, and now I've spoiled what we might've had left before you head away.' The floodgates opened and a deluge poured down her cheeks, and there was nothing she could do to stop them.

Strong arms wrapped around her, held her close to his hard body. The rough beating of his heart against her ear echoed her own. Jackson's sharp breaths lifted strands of her hair and wafted them over her face. 'I'd like to promise I'll be back, but that'd be selfish. I honestly don't know what's ahead.'

Lifting her head just enough to see his face, she told him, 'I understand. Truly. It's not as if you lied to me. Golden Bay has never been big enough for you.'

'It will be a lot harder leaving this time than it was at eighteen. There's so much that's important to me here.' His hand rubbed circles over her shoulder blades.

She raised a pathetic chuckle. 'At eighteen you left in such a hurry you scorched the road.'

'True. If only I hadn't made that promise to Juliet.'

She pulled out of that comforting hold and slashed a hand over her wet cheeks. 'I'd better go check on Constance and Abigail.'

He looked hesitant.

She put him out of his misery. 'Go home, Jackson. I won't be long and then I'll be doing the same thing.' Which meant collecting Nicholas from his parents' house. This just got harder and harder.

'Jess…' He hesitated. 'It might be in both our interests if I leave for Asia sooner than I'd planned.'

She gasped. She hadn't seen that coming. 'What about Virginia? She'll be upset.'

Wincing, he replied, 'I'll talk to her, explain, hopefully make her understand. After all, it was Mum who taught me to be honest and to live by my beliefs. But I will come home often, no more staying away for years on end.'

She had no answer to that. Her heart ached so badly it felt as though it was disintegrating inside her chest. 'Will I see you before you go?'

Shock widened his eyes, tightened his mouth. He reached for her, took her shoulders and tugged her close. 'Most definitely. I won't walk away without saying goodbye.'

For the second time since he'd turned up here she spun away and put space between them. Goodbye? A cruel word. A harsh reality for her future. A bleak future without Jackson in it. Behind her the truck door slammed shut and the engine turned over. She didn't look as he drove away. If she did she'd have started running, chasing the truck, begging him to stop and talk to her some more.

She didn't even know his feelings for her. Somewhere along the way she'd started to think he might care for her a lot, even love her a little. Not that knowing would have changed what happened, but it might've been a slight salve for her battered heart.

At seven o'clock on Tuesday morning Jess woke with a thumping headache. The alarm was loud in her quiet bedroom. She'd lain awake until about four then drifted into a fitful sleep. Now all she wanted to do was stick her head under the covers and go back to sleep, where she wouldn't notice Jackson leaving.

'Mummy, I got myself up.' Nicholas bounced onto her bed, creating havoc inside her skull.

'Good for you, sweetheart. What are you going to have for breakfast today?' She wouldn't be able to swallow a thing. When would her appetite return?

'Toast with honey. Can I cook it by myself?'

That had her sitting up too fast, her head spinning like a cricket ball in flight. 'Wait until I'm out there with you.' Slipping into her heavy robe, she tied the belt at her waist and followed him out to the kitchen.

While Nicholas made toast, along with the usual mess,

she drank a cup of tea that threatened to come back up any moment.

A knock on the back door sent Nicholas rushing to open it. 'Mummy, it's Jackson.'

She tried to stand up, she really did, but her legs failed her. Her hands gripped her mug of tea as her eyes tracked Jackson as he entered the room and came towards her. Dressed in superbly cut trousers and jacket, he looked like something out of a glossy magazine, not the man in shorts and T-shirt she'd been knocking around with for the last couple of months.

'Jess.'

'Jackson.'

He'd dropped in last night to tell her he was flying out today, bound for Auckland, and on to Hong Kong on Saturday. Said it was for the best. That's what she'd spent most of the night trying to figure out—how could it be good for him or for her?

'Jackson, I made my own breakfast.' Nicholas seemed impervious to the mood in the room.

'That's great.' He looked down at her boy, and swallowed. 'Nicholas, I'm leaving today, going back to where I live.'

Her eyes blurred, her hands were like claws around the mug. *Give me strength.*

Nicholas stared up at the man he'd come to accept as part of his life. 'You can't. I don't want you to. Mummy, tell him to stay.'

There were tears in Jackson's eyes as he hunkered down to be on Nicholas's level and reached for him. 'I'm sorry, sport, but I have to go.'

'No, you don't.' Nicholas began crying, big hiccupping sobs that broke her heart as much as Jackson's leaving would.

'Can I send you emails? You can answer, telling me how your swimming lessons are going, how many fish you catch with Grady?' Sniff, sniff. Jackson studied her boy like he was storing memories to take with him.

Nicholas nodded slowly then his eyes widened in panic. 'I don't know how to email. Mummy?'

'I'll show you.' Was it a good idea to let these two stay in touch? Would Nicholas feel let down, or would he slowly get over Jackson's disappearance?

Jackson stood, Nicholas in his arms. 'I want you to look after Mummy, for me. She's very special, you know.'

Stay and look out for me yourself. 'That doesn't give you licence to do what you like around here, Nicholas.' Her smile was warped, but at least it was a smile.

'What's licence?'

'I think your mother means you can't do whatever you like without permission.' Jackson squeezed him close then dropped a kiss on his head before handing him to her. 'See you later, alligator.' His voice broke and he turned away.

She cuddled her little boy, comforting him, comforting herself. 'Ssh, sweetheart. It's going to be all right.' Like hell it would be, and now she'd lied to Nicholas. She kissed the top of his head. 'Jackson, you'd better go.' *Before I nail you to the floor so you can't. Before I fall apart, the way my boy is.* 'Please,' she begged.

He turned back to face her. 'Sure.' But he didn't move. Just stood there, watching her, sadness oozing out of those beautiful green eyes.

'Go. Now. Please.'

He stepped up beside her, his hand took her chin and gently tilted her head back. His kiss was so gentle it hurt. Her lips moulded to his, fitted perfectly, for the last time.

She breathed in to get her last taste of him, a scent to hold onto and remember in the dark of the night.

And then he was gone. Her back door closed quietly behind him. Nicholas howled louder. Jess sat there, unable to move, and let the tears flow.

Jackson had gone.

CHAPTER TEN

JESS PULLED THE bedcovers up to her chin and listened to the rain beating down on the roof. It hadn't let up all night. She'd never heard rain like it. And according to the radio it wasn't about to stop.

'Heavy rain warnings for the Cobb Valley and lower Takaka' had been the dire message, again and again.

'Not a lot I can do about it. Might as well stay snug in bed. At least until Nicholas decides he wants up and about.' The rain suited her mood. The mood that had hung over her, keeping her gripped in misery, for the two days since Jackson had walked out of her life.

It was time to get over that. Yeah, okay, time to paste a smile on her face and pretend everything was fine in her world. Going around looking like someone had stolen her house when she hadn't been looking didn't help. Starting from now, she'd enjoy these quiet moments before Nicholas demanded her attention. She flicked the bedside light on and reached for her book. 'Bliss,' she pretended.

The light flickered. Dimmed, came back to full strength. Went off.

'So much for that idea.'

'Mummy, it's gone dark,' Nicholas yelled from his bedroom. 'I'm getting up.'

'Me, too, Sweetheart.' Jess leapt out of bed and quickly

dressed in old jeans and T-shirt. It didn't matter that she looked like a tramp; Jackson wasn't around to notice. The familiar tug of need twisted at her heart, tightened her tummy. She missed him. So much. Let's face it, she'd already been missing him before he'd left.

The moment he'd said goodbye and walked away she'd shut down, squashing hard on the pain threatening to break her apart. She'd gone through the last two days at work like a robot. One day she'd have to face up to the end of her affair with Jackson, and deal with it. But right now it was a case of getting through the minutes one at a time.

With a smile on her face. No matter how false that was.

'Hey, Mummy. Can I go outside and jump in the puddles?' Nicholas appeared in her doorway, dressed in his favourite shirt—his fishing one, of course.

Another tug at her heart. At least she could be thankful that after his first outburst of disappointment Nicholas hadn't been as sad as she'd expected. But that could be because her son didn't get what goodbye really meant. Up until now anyone who said that to him always came back—from Nelson, from school, from just about anywhere. But not from Hong Kong.

'Let me see what it's like outside first. There's been a lot of rain and those puddles might be very deep.'

Jackson would still be in Auckland. He'd left Golden Bay with days to spare before the first flight he could get to Asia, running out as though dogs had been snapping at his gorgeous butt. He was staying with an old med-school pal he'd kept in touch with over the years since graduation. Or so Sasha had told her as she'd handed Jess the tissue box. There'd been a lot of tissues used in the past two days. Who'd have believed one person could produce so many tears? She could probably singlehandedly meet Golden Bay's salt requirements.

Pulling the curtains back, Jess stared at the sight of her front yard with puddles the size of small swimming pools. A trickle of concern had her heading out the front door to check what was happening with her neighbours and the road. Wet, wet, wet. Water was everywhere, and rising. She'd never seen anything like this. It looked like her house had been transplanted into the sea.

Back inside, she reached for her cellphone. At least that was working. 'Hey, Grady, just checking everything's all right over your way. We're inundated with water here. The power's out as well.'

Grady sounded calm as he told her, 'Sasha and I are with Ian and Virginia. Might be a good idea for you and Nicholas to join us. The area is copping huge runoff from the hills. That's probably what you're getting. About an hour ago it started coming across the farms, over the road and through the properties on this side.'

'I'm sure we're safe but, yeah, I might come over before it gets worse. I don't want to be stuck here with Nicholas. At the moment he thinks this is all for his benefit but if we have to wade out it won't be pretty.' Besides, there was safety in numbers and all that.

'Take your phone and call if you think you're going to get stuck. Actually, no. Stay there. I'll come and get you in the four-wheel drive. That little hybrid thing of yours won't stand a chance if there's more than a few inches of water on the road.' Click, and Grady had gone.

'Nicholas, put a jersey and your shoes in a bag. Get your rain jacket and gumboots ready too. Grady's coming to pick us up.'

'Ye-es, Grady's coming.' He leapt up and down all the

way down the hall to the laundry, where his bag hung on the back of the door.

Quickly stuffing some warm clothes in another bag for herself, she slipped into her heavy-duty jacket and went around making sure all light switches were off and everything was locked up tight. Then she grabbed another handful of Nicholas's clothes. There was no way her boy would stay dry today. Too much temptation outside.

'Nicholas…' She waited until she had his full attention. 'When we get to Mrs Wilson's you are not to go outside. It's dangerous out there. Do you understand?'

'Yes, Mummy.' He looked so innocent that she crossed her fingers. But thanks to Jackson he was more amenable these days.

Jackson. What she wouldn't do to have him walking in the front door right now.

'Grady's here.' Nicholas raced for the door to drag the poor guy inside.

Once aboard the four-wheel drive, she told Grady, 'Thanks for taking us to your in-laws'. I didn't fancy hanging around watching that water getting higher by the minute.' Mentally she crossed fingers that her house would be safe.

'No problem. The situation's going to get worse before it's over.'

Less than an hour later Jess heard from the police that her house had a torrent of water pouring through it, as did the other few houses in her immediate neighbourhood, including Mrs Harrop's place. Thankfully the old lady had gone to Nelson for a few days. The cop told her, 'Half a kilometre back the road has been undermined with a deep and wide cut made by the force of the ever-increasing volume of water. That caused it to build up and surge forward through your area.'

Her heart sank. 'At least we're safe. Thank goodness Grady came and got us.' But what about her home? All her things? Nicholas's favourite toys and books? Tears spurted down her cheeks. 'They are only possessions,' she muttered, slashing at her cheeks with the back of her hand. 'But this has turned into the week from hell.'

Sasha hugged her. 'Those things are *your* things. I get it. It isn't fair. Maybe it won't be as bad as you think.'

Jess looked at her friend and shook her head. 'You reckon?'

Then Ian burst in through his back door yelling, 'The water levels are rising fast. I need to shift the sheep out of the orchard into the yard around the house. All hands on deck.'

Virginia said, 'I'll look after Melanie and Nicholas while you're all outside.'

Sasha yelled down the phone. 'Jackson, get your butt back home. You're needed. The whole area is flooded. It's serious.'

His heart stalled. 'Is Jess all right? Nicholas?' He looked around the crowded bar, found the TV screen. A rerun of last night's rugby game between the Auckland Blues and the Hawkes Bay Magpies was in full swing. He needed the news channel. 'What about Mum and Dad? I know you said the house was high and dry, but how are they dealing with this?' The orchard had gone under water before but they'd always pulled through. Of course, they hadn't been dealing with other things like MS before. But Jess? How would she fare? Her house was closer to the hills. *Oh, God, Jess, I've let you down.*

Sasha ramped up her yelling. 'Mum and Dad are great. It's Jessica who needs you. Her house's been flooded.

She's probably lost just about everything. Including you, you big moron.'

The expletives spitting out of his mouth copped him a few unwanted glares from people sitting at the next table. For a moment he'd forgotten he was in the pub. Up until five minutes ago he'd been having a quiet beer and early brunch with his friend Simon from med-school days and pretending everything was okay. Now he couldn't deny it any longer. He shouldn't be here. Neither should he be going to Hong Kong. 'Tell me about Jess. Is she safe?' His heart finally started working properly and he could hardly hear for the thumping in his ears.

'She's out helping rescue people, patching others up, making sure they've got somewhere to go for the duration of the flood.'

Typical, big-hearted Jess. The woman he hadn't had the courage to tell he loved her. Jackson stood up abruptly, his chair crashing back. He needed to see the flood for himself, to get a grip on reality. 'Has this been on the news?'

'Where have you been, Jackson?' Sasha sounded completely fed up with him. As she had every right to be. He'd been an idiot, thinking he could walk away from them all. Especially from Jess, the love of his life.

'What's up, Jackson?' Simon stood up too, righted the chair and apologised to the people sitting behind them.

'I need to get the bar owner to change to the news channel. It's flooding at home. Badly.' With the phone still glued to his ear, he began picking his way through the crowd.

Simon grabbed his elbow. 'You want to get us lynched? Every single person in this bar has their eyes fixed to that game.'

'Tough. This is important.'

'That's all relative. Come with me. I have a better idea. Besides, I want to live a while longer yet.' Simon was nothing if not persistent. Jackson's elbow was grabbed in something resembling a rugby hold and he was quick-marched outside.

'Where are we going?' he demanded, as fury began roaring up inside him. 'I need to see the news channel.'

'What did you say?' Sasha demanded in his ear.

He'd forgotten all about his sister. 'Sorry, Sasha. Got to go. Simon's dragging me halfway around the city and I need to stop him.'

'Whatever. I got it wrong, didn't I?' Sasha sounded disappointed—in him.

'Got what wrong?' He tugged free of Simon's grip, then stopped as understanding hit. They were outside an appliance store. A store where hopefully someone would listen to his request. 'Thanks, Simon.'

'I thought you cared.' Sasha spoke so softly he nearly missed her words. 'I've got to go. We're dealing with an emergency down here.'

'Wait. Sasha, please. Is the road over the hill a go?'

'Nope. Landslides closed it around lunchtime.'

Jackson opened his mouth to swear again, glanced around the store and saw the row of televisions—all playing the news. Showing Golden Bay like he'd never seen it before. Showing his home town besieged by water. 'Crap.'

Water ran amok, taking trees and kennels and dead cattle with it. Brown, swirling water decimating every-thing in its path. Suddenly the only place on earth he wanted to be was in Golden Bay, in the thick of it, with Jess, helping her while she helped everyone else. And it had taken a damned disaster to wake him up to that fact.

Simon said, 'I'll run you to the airport.'

'I'll have to hire a private plane when I get to Nelson.' Hell, he hoped he could get on a commercial flight from Auckland to Nelson at such short notice. He didn't fancy the extra hour and a half by road if he had to land in Blenheim. He wouldn't consider the time delay if Christchurch was his only option.

Five hours later Jackson dumped his bags in the corner of the Pohara Motor Camp office and headed for the communal kitchen/dining room being used as an emergency centre. The moment he walked through the door his eyes scanned for Jess, came up blank.

'Where's Jess?' he demanded the instant he saw Grady.

'Hello to you, too. She's seeing to Sam. He's injured himself while trying to dig a ditch to divert water from the house.' Grady reached for a ringing phone. 'She's fine, Jackson.'

Jackson picked his way around people and bags and boxes of food, heading for the white board on the wall. Lists scrolled down the board. Properties damaged by the flood, people being evacuated, injured folk needing house calls. He'd seen some sad sights on his way in from Takaka airstrip, travelling first by four-wheel drive then by boat and lastly on foot.

Jess's house was listed in the flooded properties, as was her other place, where Mrs Harrop lived. Yet Jess was out there doing what she did best—looking out for others. She was magnificent. And he'd been going to walk away. Idiot. He wanted to run to her, stick by her while she went about her calls. But she'd hate that. Anyway, he could be put to better use, attending patients himself.

Impatience gripped him as he waited for Grady to finish his call. Sounded like someone out past Pohara needed urgent attention from a medic. 'I'll go,' he announced the moment Grady hung up.

'Take my truck. There's a medical kit and hopefully anything else you'll need inside. Tom Gregory, Tarakohe, had his arm squashed while trying to tie his fishing boat down.'

Jackson snatched the keys flying towards him. 'I'll be in touch.'

'Good, because I've already got another call for you out at Wainui Inlet after you're done with Tom.'

Jess shivered. Under her thick jacket her clothes were soaked through. On her way to the truck that she'd hijacked from Ian she'd slipped in the mud and gone into a ditch to be submerged in sludge. It would be weeks before the foul taste of mud left her mouth.

It was well after seven and as dark as coal. This had been the longest day of her life, and it wasn't anywhere near over. Too many people needed help for her to put her feet up in front of Virginia's fire. But what she wouldn't give for a hot chocolate right about now.

Not going to happen. If she was lucky she'd get a lukewarm coffee and a droopy sandwich at Pohara before heading out somewhere else. She wouldn't be the only one feeling exhausted. All the emergency crews had been working their butts off throughout the day. The damage out there was horrendous, taking its toll on people, animals and buildings.

Buildings. As in houses. Her home.

No. She wasn't going to think about that. Wasn't going to consider the damage she'd seen briefly when the police had taken her home to collect some things. At least she'd managed to grab some clothes, a few photos and a couple of Nicholas's favourite toys. The rest didn't bear thinking about.

Hunched over the steering-wheel to peer through the murk and hoping like crazy the vehicle stayed on the road, she drove cautiously towards the temporary emergency centre. Shivering with cold, yawning with fatigue, it was hard to concentrate.

Focus. The last thing the emergency guys needed was her driving into a ditch and having to be rescued.

Finally she pulled up outside the well-lit building, got out and immediately pushed open the door. If she sat still she'd fall asleep. She'd fall asleep walking if she wasn't careful.

The heat exploded as she stepped through the door into the chaos of emergency rescue. Hesitating while her eyes adjusted to the bright lights, she could feel her hands losing their grip on the medical bag she'd brought inside to replenish. She heard it hit the floor with a sickening thud and couldn't find the energy to bend down and pick it up again.

Someone caught her, led her to a chair and gently pushed her down. A cup of tea appeared on the table in front of her. 'Get that inside you, Jess. I bet you didn't stop for lunch.'

Her stomach rumbled in answer. Lunch. What was that? 'The store was shut.' She'd never get that cup to her lips without spilling most of the contents.

'I'll get you a sandwich.'

The rumble was louder this time. She blinked. Looked up at this kind apparition hovering over her. That's when she knew she'd lost her mind. Exhaustion had caught up, obviously tipping her over the edge of sanity. She dropped her eyes, focused on the cup until it was very clear in her mind, no blurring at the edges of her sight. Looking up again, her breath snagged in the back of her throat. Jackson? If this was what not eating did then she'd schedule meals every hour from now on. Seeing Jackson at every turn would put her in the loony bin.

'Hey, sweetheart, you need to eat while Sheree finds you some warm, dry clothes.' A lopsided smile kept her from looking away.

Funny how her lungs seemed to have gone on strike. 'Is it really you?' How could it be? He should be somewhere over Australia by now. The tremors that had been racking her turned into quakes that would knock the socks off the Richter scale.

'Yes, it's me. I'm home, Jess. For good.' Steady hands held the cup to her lips. 'Now get some of this inside you.'

Her lips were numb with cold and the liquid dribbled down her chin, but some ran over her tongue and down her throat. It was good, sending some warmth into the chill. She took another mouthful, this time most of it going in the right direction. 'Define "for good",' she croaked.

'As in for the next fifty years at least.'

She couldn't do the sums. Her brain was struggling with drinking tea, let alone anything else. But she figured he meant he'd be here for a long while. 'Great.'

Now she really looked at him, concentrating as hard as she had while driving from Sam's. Really, really saw the man hunkered down in front of her, those beautiful deep green eyes fixed on her. Need laced that gaze. So did apology. And concern. Could that be love lingering around the edges, too? Or was she hallucinating?

'I heard your home has taken a hit.'

Oh. Not love. Just everyday concern for someone he knew well. That gave her the strength to murmur, 'Got a bulldozer out in your dad's shed? I'm going to need it.'

Her lips pressed together, holding back her returning bewilderment. This was too much. First her home had been all but destroyed. And now the man who had walked away from her two days ago, taking her heart with him, was in front of her, his hand on her knee, looking like he… Like he… That was the problem. She didn't understand any of this. Why had he suddenly reappeared?

Whatever the reason, she really didn't need this right now. She was busy helping folk in the bay. It was what she needed to do, it was how she atoned for being a brat teenager. Had she been even more badly behaved as a young woman than she'd imagined? Was that why all this was happening to her? Would she never pay for her mistakes?

On a long, steadying breath, she told Jackson, 'Glad you're here. They need all the medics they can get.'

'I've been helping for the last four hours. Seems we're all caught up for a while.' He took the plate of sandwiches Sheree arrived with and handed her one. 'Eat.'

'Your jersey's wet.' So was his hair. She hadn't noticed.

'Last time I looked, it was still raining.'

'I need to top up my bag.' Chew, chew. Concentrating on more than one thing at a time was too hard right now.

'I'll see to it in a minute.' He didn't move.

'Jackson,' she growled around another mouthful of bread and ham. 'Why are you here?'

'Because I couldn't leave.' He pulled another chair around and sat in front of her, still holding the plate of sandwiches. 'I was wrong to think I could go, Jess. No, let me rephrase that. I knew I wanted to stay but that bloody promise kept getting in the way, doing my head in.'

Chew, chew. 'Okay.' Was it? Jackson was back, whatever that meant.

'Jackson,' Grady called. 'Got a minute? We've got a

young boy needing stitches in his hand waiting in the other room.'

'Sure.' Leaning close, he kissed her cheek so softly she probably imagined it. 'Don't go anywhere.'

Jess watched him stride to the back door and remove his sodden jacket before heading down the hall to the bathroom. 'Did I just see Jackson in here?' she whispered.

Sheree placed a pile of clothes on the chair beside her. 'Definitely Jackson. No one else around here looks so cute in his city clobber, even when it looks like he's been swimming in it.'

'That's because no one else around here wears city clothes.' But Sheree was right. He looked downright gorgeous. Sexy and hot and warm and caring. Even when he was so bedraggled. Jackson. Had he brought her heart back to put her all together?

'Why has he come back?' she asked no one in particular.

'Go and change into those dry clothes, Jess. They'll be too big for you but at least you'll feel warmer.' Sheree could be bossy when she put her mind to it. 'Jackson isn't going anywhere tonight. You'll get your answer, I'm sure.'

Who'd have believed tears would feel so hot when your cheeks were frozen?

CHAPTER ELEVEN

JACKSON TRIED TO watch Jess as she carefully drove the short distance to his parents' place, avoiding racing water as best she could, driving around fallen trees and bobbing logs. Why had she insisted on driving when she was shattered? Trying to regain some control? Over herself? Or him?

He could barely see her outline in the dark but as they'd pulled away from the emergency centre he'd noted how tight her mouth was, how white her lips were. Her eyes had stood out in her pale face. Worry had turned their warm brown shade to burnt coffee. Now her fingers were wrapped around the steering-wheel so hard he thought he'd be peeling them off for her when they stopped.

'You're staring.'

Yes, he was. Drinking in the dark shape of her in the gloom. She was all mussed, her damp hair fizzing in all directions. Adorable. He'd only been gone a couple of days but he'd missed her every single second of the time. He'd had to fight himself not to return. How bloody stupid was that? Thought he knew what he was doing? Yeah, right. Think again, buddy.

Her voice squeaked as she asked, 'How did you get through? I heard the hill's closed.'

'Hired a plane out of Nelson. I'm glad the airstrip is on higher ground.'

'It's worse around here.'

'Shocking. I haven't seen anything like it before. The orchard's a disaster area, avocado and citrus trees standing deep in the swirling water. Fortunately the house is safe on the higher ground, unscathed by the flood, and full of people Mum and Dad are taking in and feeding.' People that included Jess and Nicholas.

'It's what people do for each other.' He thought Jess glanced at him. 'This isn't the first time this has happened in the bay.' Her tone was sharp, fed up. The turn into Dad's drive was equally sharp.

'Yeah, but I've always been somewhere else.' There lay his problem. He'd done a damned fine job of avoiding being a part of this place when the bad times were going down. Only ever here for some good times. But not any more. 'Jess, there's something I—' He jerked forward as she braked too hard for the conditions.

'Here we are. I can't wait to put on dry, clean clothes, my clothes. And to hug Nicholas.' Slam. Her door banged shut.

'No hugs for me, then.' What had he honestly expected? The band playing 'Welcome home, lover'? Jackson sat shivering from the bone chilling effect of his wet clothes and Jess's avoidance. He watched her stomping across the yard to Mum's back door. Every step sent up a spray of water. Every foot forward, away from him, accentuated the fact she couldn't deal with his return. Didn't want to, more like.

Finally he shoved the door open and dropped to the ground. Tonight wasn't the time for deep and meaningful conversations. Not when Mum and Dad's house was full of neighbours. Not when Jess had her own house situation to deal with. Not when Nicholas would want her attention.

He drew a breath and dug deep for one attribute he didn't have. Patience. Somehow he had to hold back and not rush in waving a flag, demanding that Jess listen to him. Somehow he had to take the time to show he would stand by her no matter what. Help her fix the home she'd been so proud of and that now stood full of muddy water. Wrecked. Not that anyone really knew how vast the damage would be. It'd take a few days before assessors and builders could even begin evaluating the situation.

One thing he knew with absolute certainty—whatever it took, he'd do it to win Jess's heart. For ever.

'Hey, you coming in?' Dad yelled from the back door. 'I've still got some of that bourbon left.'

'That's my dad.' His heart lifted a fraction as he went to join him. But as he approached the porch he noticed how grey Dad had turned, almost overnight. He wasn't coping with Mum's illness, and this situation would have exacerbated everything. His leaving wouldn't have helped matters either.

And I thought I could leave. His gut clenched. 'Dad, I'm sorry.' He wrapped his arms around the man who'd been there for him when he'd stubbed his toe, when he'd caught his first fish, when he'd wanted to know about sex, when he'd shouted he was leaving Golden Bay for ever. 'I'm not leaving again.'

'Tell that to Jess, not me. I'd already worked that out. Even before you had. But that young lady inside is going to take a lot more persuasion.' Dad locked gazes with him. 'She needs you, son. Badly. From what Jonty says, it's really bad news about her property. Both houses are wrecked.'

'Yeah, I saw that on the board at Pohara.' No wonder Jess didn't have time for him.

Dad nodded. 'You're onto it.'

The bottom dropped out of Jackson's stomach. He should be shot. He'd been so sure of himself, acting strong and supposedly doing the right thing. It had taken an act of nature to bring him to his senses. It was going to take a lifetime to prove to Jess he could change, and get it right the second time round. If she even gave him a chance.

Jess forced her feet forward, one slippery step at a time, through her kitchen into the lounge. The mud and sludge was above her ankles, but overnight the water had at last dropped to ground level. Everything dripped moisture. Brown goo stained the walls higher than her waist. Furniture sat like sodden hulks, ruined for ever. The smell turned her nose, curled her stomach.

On the wall photos were buckled from moisture. Seeing one of Nicholas, grinning out at her as he rode around the front lawn, snagged her heart, threatened to break her determination to be strong. She'd sneaked out of the Wilsons' home the moment it was light enough to see her hand held out in front of her. The night had been long and stressful and sleep evasive as she'd tossed and turned on the couch. She'd desperately wanted to see her house, the place she'd made into a home for her and Nicholas. A safe haven where she knew she finally belonged.

Of course she'd known it would be bad, but she had to see it, to know by touch, smell and sight just how bad it really was. She needed this short time alone to absorb it all. That way she'd be able to hold herself together and be strong in front of everyone else, no matter how generous they were with offers of help and new furniture.

Tracking through the mess, she made her way to Nicholas's room and swiped at her cheeks. So much for not crying. The quilt she'd bought at the local fair when Nicholas was two now had a distinct brown tinge but the appliquéd zoo animals were still clear, just dark brown.

'Will I ever be able to wash that clean?'

Pulling open a drawer, she gasped, still able to be surprised at the mess inside.

'Guess we're going shopping for clothes in the next few days, my boy. Thank goodness you wore your lucky fishing shirt yesterday.' The tears became a steady stream.

Another ruined photo caught her eye. How had she missed this one yesterday? There hadn't been time to collect them all, but this one? Reaching out slowly, she lifted it by the frame and stared at the excited face of Nicholas with his first fish. Jackson squatting beside him, an equally big grin on his gorgeous face.

The stream became a torrent. Jackson. Nicholas. The two most important people in her life. The life that had turned into one big mess.

'Hey.' Strong arms wrapped around her, turned her to hold her tight against that familiar, strong body she'd missed so much for the last three days. No, make that since the day she'd told Jackson she loved him.

The torrent turned into a flood, pouring onto Jackson's jersey, like the floodwaters that had soaked his clothes yesterday.

All the time she sobbed he held her against him, his hands soothing her by rubbing her back, his chin settled on the top of her head. Letting his strength soak into her. Calming her with his quiet presence. Not trying to deny that she had a problem but showing he'd be there as she sorted her way through the debris that had become her life.

Finally the tears slowed, stopped. Her heart felt lighter and yet nothing had changed. The house was still a wreck. Jackson would still return to Hong Kong. He might've said he was staying but she couldn't take a chance on that. Time to toughen up. She pulled away, moved to stand in the middle of the room, the photo still in her hand. Wiping her other hand over her cheeks, she told him, 'Thank you. As if there isn't already enough water around the place.'

Jackson winced, but he didn't turn round and hightail it out of her house. 'Let's see what we can save. Throw anything not ruined into the truck and take it back to Mum's to clean before storing. Then we'll check out Mrs Harrop's place.'

It was a plan and she desperately needed something to focus on. Nodding, she walked through to her bedroom and stared around. Looked at the bed where she'd had so much fun with Jackson. Her wardrobe door stood ajar, her shoes everywhere. Bending down, she picked up one of the apricot silk pair she'd worn at the wedding. 'Ruined. But I guess they're only shoes.'

She didn't realise Jackson had followed her until he said, 'No such thing as *only* shoes for women.' When she looked up, he gave her a coaxing smile. 'I'll take you shopping when we've had time to work out what's going to happen with all this.'

That's what she'd said about Nicholas's things. Throw 'em out and get new ones. That didn't seem so easy now. 'I'll get some bags to put things in.'

'Have you called your insurance company yet?' Jackson seemed determined to stick with her.

'Hardly. Too busy yesterday and it's still too early today.' Where were those large black bin liners? They'd be perfect for the damp clothes she needed to take away for washing.

'Jess.' Jackson stood beside her as she poked through a drawer of sodden plastic bags and cling wrap.

'Here we are.' She snatched up the roll and kneed the drawer closed.

'Jess.' A little louder. And when she turned to head to Nicholas's bedroom he put both hands on her shoulders. 'Jess, I don't know if this is the right time to tell you but I love you.'

'Right.' *He loves me. That's got to be good. But it doesn't fix a thing. I need to sort clothes and stuff before the day gets started and I have to go to work.*

Those big hands gripping her gave her a gentle shake. 'I am not going back to Hong Kong. I'm here to stay.'

'That's good. We need another doctor in the bay. Rory's busting to go live with his girlfriend in Auckland.' See, some things did work out if everyone was patient.

Her foot nudged something in the mud covering the floor. Bending down, she retrieved Nicholas's stuffed giraffe, Long Neck. The original yellow and black colours looked decidedly worse for their night in the mud. 'This is one of Nicholas's favourites.' She dropped it into one of the black bags.

Jackson took the roll of bags and tore off a couple. 'I'll deal with Nicholas's room if you like, while you go through your drawers and wardrobe.' He sounded very upbeat. Why? It wasn't like she'd acknowledged his statement.

Some time later she wound a plastic tie around the neck of the last full bag from her room and dumped it on the bed, on top of the beautiful quilt that apparently Sasha's grandmother had made years ago. Jess considered it antique and now it was destined for the trash. What a shame. Hands on hips, she stood at the end of the bed and looked around at what had been her pride and joy. She'd painted the whole place, but here in her bedroom she'd let loose with her creative side, buying beautiful little knick knacks for the top of her dressing table, bedside lamps that matched colours in the quilt and the curtains she'd made. She'd been so damned proud of those curtains and now look at them—sodden, muddy and hanging all askew.

Water dripped onto her breasts. Tears? Surely she'd run out by now. Apparently not. They didn't stop. Her hands began shaking and she had to grip her hips tight to keep them under some sort of control.

'Hey, you're crying.' Jackson suddenly appeared before her with a box of tissues that was miraculously dry. 'Here, let me.' Oh, so gently he sponged up the tears, only to have to repeat the exercise again and again.

Her bottom lip trembled. 'I know it's only little, and very ordinary, but this is my home. I made it how I wanted it to be, a place for Nicholas to grow up in feeling secure and loved. I've been happy here, settled for the very first time in my life.'

Those long, strong fingers touched her cheeks, lifted her face so she had to look into his eyes. 'You think that you've lost all that because your house is a write-off?'

Her head dipped in acknowledgement. That's what she'd been trying to say, yes.

'Sweetheart, the love that permeates this home doesn't come from the paint and curtains and flower vases and books on the shelves. It comes from in here.' He tapped her chest gently, right against her heart. 'From within you. That love goes where you go. It's who you are, and always will be. Nicholas is going to be secure and loved by you all his life, even though he mightn't grow up in this particular home. Even when he eventually heads out into the world on his own, he'll know you love him. Whether you get this place put back together or buy another one with the insurance money, it will be filled with your personality, your love, fun and laughter.'

For Jackson that had to be a record speech. She blinked as the tight knots in her tummy began letting go some tension. The trembling in her hands eased, stopped. 'You really, really think so?' she whispered.

'I know so.' His head lowered so that his mouth was close to hers. 'I really, really know.' Then he kissed her. A quiet kiss filled with understanding, with that love he'd not long ago declared, with his generosity. He was giving her something back after all that had been taken from her since the moment he'd walked out of her life three days ago. 'I love you,' he murmured against her mouth.

Jess leaned forward so that her breasts were crushed against his chest, her mouth kissed his in return, her hands finally lifted from her hips to his neck and held onto him. 'I don't know what to do. I love you so much and yet I can't ask you to stay. You hate it here.'

'I'm staying. End of story. I don't hate it here any more. You taught me what this community is all about.'

'Me? How?' Surprise rocked through her. 'All I do is try and make up for the mistakes I made when I was young and in need of friends who'd love me.'

'Jess, Jess, you don't get it. Yesterday, when you were dealt a blow here, what did you do? Stand around bemoaning your bad luck? Not likely. You went out caring for other people. That's community spirit in spades.'

'I'm a nurse. That's what nurses do.'

And right on cue her work phone beeped. 'Jessica, I think my waters just broke.'

'Lynley? Is that you?'

'Yes. Ouch. That wasn't nice. I'm having some light pains every ten minutes or so. Guess this is it. Do I go to the centre now?'

A grim smile twisted her mouth. 'You can wait until those contractions are closer, about six minutes between them. Unless it's going to be difficult getting there after yesterday's flood, then I'd suggest making your way there now.' It was going to take some effort for her to get there given the road this side of town had been underwater last night.

'It's a clear run from here. What about you?' Lynley asked.

'I'll be there as soon as possible. You concentrate on that baby's arrival.' She closed the phone and glanced at Jackson, to find him watching her closely.

'Guess we're headed for town, then. Have you got time to pick up some breakfast from Mum's first?'

'The baby's not rushing but I have no idea if the road is manageable.' And why are you coming with me?

'Let's go and find out.' He took the bags of clothes she'd dumped on the bed and headed out to the truck he'd borrowed.

Nothing else for her to do but follow.

When Jackson had seen Jess's shocked reaction to the state of her home he had wanted to pick her up, hold her close and transport her away from it all. He'd wanted to run her a hot bubble bath and let her soak away her desolation. Not that she'd have let him if he'd even tried. Had she heard him say he loved her? Really heard? Or had his declaration been like words on the wind? Not connecting with her?

He'd been disappointed at her lack of reaction but he figured it had been the wrong time. At least, if she knew how he felt she'd know she wasn't on her own with this. Not that she was. Mum and Dad had had to be restrained from rushing over the moment they'd known where she'd gone this morning. Only by explaining that he'd be helping Jess and that he wanted to tell her why he was home had he managed to make them stay put.

He pressed some numbers on his phone, got hold of Jonty at the fire station. 'Hey, man, how's our road this morning? Is it passable? Jess has a patient in labour in town.'

'It's open but slippery as hell. There's a temporary fix where the road was washed away. Don't let her drive that thing she calls a car. It won't hold on the tarmac.'

'That thing, as you put it, has been submerged most of the night. It's not going anywhere.' He didn't know if Jess had looked in her garage yet, and he'd try to keep her out of there for now.

Jonty groaned. 'Jess has had more than her share of knocks in this flood.'

'She sure has. I'm heading in with her so if anyone needs a doctor over the next few hours I'll be at the medical centre.' He snapped the phone shut, went to find Jess. 'Road's open so let's grab some breakfast and take it with us. We can leave those bags of your belongings at the house.' Mum would probably have everything washed by the time Jess got back.

'You're coming with me? It's a normal birth, Jackson.'

'Sure, but I might be of use at the centre. Besides, there're enough people milling around at home to drive me to drink. It's too soon to start clearing the orchards, so I'm superfluous.' I want to be with you, supporting you, because I don't believe you're totally back on your feet as far as the shock is concerned.

She flicked him a brief smile. 'You're starting to think like a local. You know that?'

'If you'd said that two months ago I'd have run for the hills.'

'Didn't you do just that three days ago? Figuratively speaking.' Those eyes that always got to him were totally focused on him right now.

'Guilty as charged.' His stomach clenched, relaxed. Of course she'd want to take a crack at him. He'd hurt her by leaving like he had. Somehow he was going to make that up to her. But he wasn't barrelling in on this one. They had their whole lives ahead of them. He'd take it slower than he was used to doing with anything.

Parking outside Mum and Dad's house, he pulled on the handbrake. 'I'll tell you something. What you just said about me thinking like a local made me feel warm and fuzzy, not cold and panicked. Guess I'm improving.'

Jess actually chuckled. There was even a hint of mischief in her eyes. 'Watch this space. You'll be standing for mayor before we know it.'

'Get outta here.' Not that Golden Bay had a mayor. There were plenty of people who liked to think they were running the district, but official business was down over the hill.

'Don't let me forget my kit.' She dropped to the ground and reached into the back for two bags. 'Wonder if any of the beach houses are vacant.'

'You thinking of renting one for a while?'

She nodded. 'Got to find somewhere to live fairly quickly.'

Now he had something practical he could do for the woman he loved. 'Leave it with me. I'll ring round, or go online, while you're bringing that baby into this wet world.'

Her gaze lit up as she looked skyward. 'The sun's peeking out, most of the sky's blue, and the rain has stopped everywhere.'

And Jess had started looking a tiny bit more relaxed. Relief nearly made him swing her up in his arms to kiss her soft lips. But as his foot came off the ground to move towards her, caution held him back. Patience, man, patience. Do not rush her. Not today, anyway. He smiled and lifted out two more heavy bags of damp belongings before following that gorgeous butt inside.

Virginia handed her a steaming mug of tea even before she'd got her boots off. 'Here you go, Jess. Get that in you. I tried to get you to have one before you left at sun-up but you weren't hearing anything.'

Jess apologised. 'I had my mind on my home, nothing else.'

'That's what I thought.' Virginia's arm draped around her shoulders. 'You and Nicholas stay here for as long as it takes to sort everything out. No arguments.'

'I'm not arguing. I'm just too exhausted to do anything much about finding somewhere to live today. So, thanks very much.' She laid her cheek against the other woman's arm for a moment, absorbing the warmth and care. 'Thank you,' she whispered again.

Jackson strolled through the farmhouse-sized kitchen and smiled at her and his mother. 'We're heading into town shortly. Anyone here who needs to go that way?' He was definitely sounding more and more like most of the other caring people in the district.

Virginia dropped her arm and handed Jackson a mug. 'Not that I know of. Want to take some food with you? Can't imagine any shops being open today.'

Ten minutes later Jess sat in the passenger seat watching Jackson skilfully negotiate a small washout just past her house. 'It could take months to get everything back to normal.'

Her work phone buzzed in her pocket. 'Hey, Lynley, that you?'

'My contractions are down to five minutes apart and we're waiting at the birthing unit.'

'Nearly there.' She closed the phone. 'That girl is so calm for a first baby.'

'What were you like when you had Nicholas?'

'Terrible. My baby was the first baby ever to be born. No one could've possibly understood what I was going through. I'm surprised I had any friends left by the time I'd finished.' She grinned. 'Labour hurts, big time. And mine went on for thirty-one hours. I swear it's the only time Nicholas has been late for anything.'

'Would you do it again?'

Talk about a loaded question. 'You going somewhere with this?'

'Yep.' He slowed behind a tractor towing a trailer laden with broken trees. Driving patiently, he kept back from the mud sent into the air by the trailer wheels. 'I'd love to have kids.'

And that had something to do with her? Though he had said he loved her—three times. 'Yeah, I'd do it again. The pain's quickly forgotten when you hold your baby in your arms for the first time.'

Jackson didn't say any more, just concentrated on getting them through the mud and debris littering what used to be a perfectly good road.

The medical centre was surprisingly quiet. 'I think everyone's too busy cleaning up to be bothered with visiting us,' Mike theorised, when they tramped inside with their plastic box of breakfast.

'Where are Lynley and Trevor?' she asked.

'Over in the maternity wing.'

Jackson continued walking through the centre. 'I'm over there if you find you're suddenly rushed off your feet, Mike.'

'You don't have to come with me.' Jess hurried after Jackson.

'I'll make breakfast.'

'You have an answer for everything,' she muttered under her breath.

He leaned close, placed a soft kiss on her cheek. 'Better get used to that.'

Lynley had already changed into a loose-fitting hospital gown. 'Can't stand anything constricting me at the moment,' she told Jess the moment she turned into the birthing room. 'Ahh, Trevor, hold me.' Her pretty face contorted as vice-like pain caught her.

Trevor stood rock solid as his wife clung to him, his hands around her waist. 'Glad you got through, Jess. I heard about your place being flooded. Hope it's going to be all right. If there's anything I can do, give me a call, okay?'

'Thanks. It's too soon to know what'll happen with it. This is Jackson Wilson. He's an emergency doctor and, no, Lynley you're not having an emergency.'

Jackson waved a hand at the couple. 'If you don't want me hanging around just say so, otherwise I'm here to watch and learn.'

When the contraction had passed Jess indicated for Lynley to sit back on the bed and then wrapped the blood-pressure cuff around the mother-to-be's arm. 'Baseline obs first and then I'll listen to baby's heartbeat.'

'Any idea how long this is going to take?' Lynley asked.

'It's like the piece of string. Every baby is different. Your BP's good.' She listened through the stethoscope to the baby's heartbeats, counting silently. 'All good there, too.'

'Now we wait, right?' Trevor said.

'We certainly do. And be grateful that wee boy didn't decide yesterday was the day to arrive.' Jess sat on a low stool and filled in patient observations.

Jackson said, 'I'll make our breakfast. Can I get you anything Lynley? Trevor?'

Another contraction, and again Trevor held Lynley. And again. Jackson returned from the kitchen with a tray laden with toast and jam, and four cups of coffee. More contractions, more observations noted on the page. The morning groaned past and Lynley began to get tired.

'I'm fed up with this pain,' she yelled once.

'Why did you get me pregnant?' she demanded of Trevor another time. 'Do you know what you're putting me through?'

Jess sympathised, while thinking that at least Lynley hadn't resorted to swearing at the poor guy, like some women did.

Jackson stood behind her and rubbed her back when she rose from the stool. How did he know she ached just there? And did he understand he was knocking down her resistance towards him?

Finally, some time after three o'clock, Lynley suddenly announced, 'I want to push. Now.' She sank onto the bed and leaned back against the stack of pillows Jackson had placed there earlier in case she got tired of standing.

'Let me take a look at you.' Jess pulled on another pair of gloves and squatted on her stool again. 'Push when you're ready. There you go. The head has appeared. Keep pushing, Lynley. That's it. You're doing brilliantly.'

Lynley's attention was focused entirely on pushing her baby out into the world.

Then the baby slipped out into Jess's waiting hands. 'Welcome to the world, baby Coomes.' Jess wiped the little boy's mouth clear of fluid and draped him over his mother's breasts.

'Oh, my goodness. Look at him, Trevor. He's perfect.' Tears streamed down the new mother's cheeks. 'Didn't we do great?'

Trevor was grinning and crying, staring at his son like he was the most amazing sight ever.

Which he was. Jess blinked rapidly. It didn't matter how many babies she'd delivered, today baby Coomes was the most special. Next week there'd be another for her to get all soppy over.

'Isn't that the most beautiful sight?' Jackson spoke quietly beside her, emotion making his voice raw.

Maybe he really did mean to settle down here. 'It is. Once I've dealt with the cord and afterbirth let's take a break and give these two time alone with their son before the families descend. There'll be no peace when they all arrive.' Which was why Lynley had said right from the outset she didn't want anyone knowing she was in labour.

Mike had locked up the medical centre and gone home, no doubt crossing his fingers he'd get a few hours to himself and his wife, Roz. Today everyone's focus would be on clean-up and less on health issues. Tomorrow might be different as reality settled in.

Jess switched on the lights in the kitchen and filled the kettle for a cup of tea. She automatically got out two cups. Then she found the tin of chocolate biscuits Sasha kept hidden in her locker and sprang the lid, quickly stuffing a biscuit in her mouth. 'I need sugar.'

Pulling out a chair, Jackson sat and sprawled his long legs half across the room. 'You must be exhausted. Did you sleep much last night?'

'Next to nothing. My mind would not shut down.'

'I've found three houses for rent that you can look at. Two at Pohara and one at Para Para. You can see see them any time you want. You've got first dibs on all three.'

Leaning back against the bench top, she folded her arms under her breasts. 'Para Para would be lovely. That long, wide, sweeping beach is stunning, though a bit dangerous for Nicholas when it's windy. Which is often.'

'Not too far out of town?'

'Unfortunately, yes. So I'm already down to two.' She gave him a tired smile. 'Thank you for doing this. I do appreciate it.'

'Just want to help.'

Her forefingers scratched at her sleeves. He'd told her he loved her and she hadn't said a word. Yet he hadn't stalked off in a sulk. Far from it, he'd stayed by her side all day. Helping with the birth, making endless rounds of sandwiches and coffee, looking up rental properties, rubbing her back when it got sore.

Raising her head from where she'd been staring at the tips of her running shoes that were never used for running, she looked directly at him and said, 'Jackson, I love you, too.' When he made to stand up she held up a hand. 'But that doesn't mean I'm going to do anything about it.'

It hurt just to say the words. A deep hurt that twisted in her stomach. She wanted him so much, would do almost anything to give in and accept his love and make a life with him.

'Want to elaborate, Jess?' he asked, bewilderment lacing his tone.

'My parents.' This was hard. So hard. 'They love each other very much.' Too much. 'To the point they are selfish with it.' They don't even realise it. 'They excluded me from a lot. Anything that money couldn't buy, really.' Her eyesight blurred. 'Yes, I love you, Jackson. But what if I love you so much I cut Nicholas out of the picture, forget to give him hugs and kisses, miss school plays, send him on expensive holidays to get him out of the way?' Her voice had got quieter and quieter until she could barely hear herself. 'You want kids, but what if I neglect them, too?'

'You won't.' Two little words and yet there was the power of conviction in them. 'I know you, Jessica Baxter. I've seen you with Nicholas. You totally love him. You'd never be able to avoid hugging him. You'll never want to miss seeing his first proper fish.'

'You're missing the point.' That had been when it had only been her and Nicholas, before she went so far as to admit Jackson into her life properly.

'No.' He stood up and reached for her. With his arms around her waist he leaned back and looked down into her eyes. '*You're* missing the point. You're a natural mother. You'll never be otherwise. But you've got a big heart, Jess, big enough for me as well. And for our children, if we have them. You can love us all. You do love Nicholas and me already. What has Nicholas missed out on since that very first night when we went to bed together? Go on. Tell me.' His mouth was smiling, like this wasn't the issue she'd believed it was. His eyes were brimming with love for her.

'I can't think of anything.' Nicholas certainly seemed

as happy as ever when Jackson was around. In fact, he loved Jackson and the things they had done together.

'Do you trust me to give you a nudge if I think you're not getting the mix right? Because I certainly would. But, Jess, I don't believe it will ever come to that.'

He truly believed she wasn't like her parents. Wow. 'I do love you both and I hoped I was getting it right. But it's hard to know. Mum and Dad don't have a clue what they've excluded me from. They honestly believe they've been great parents.'

'I know you're an awesome parent. I wouldn't want anyone else to be my children's mother.' Jackson lowered his head, his lips finding hers. His kiss, when it came, was tender and loving and understanding, and it fired up her passion. 'I love you, Jess. Will you take a chance and marry me? We could have so many babies you'd always be inundated with their demands, and I'll be making arrangements for date nights so I can have you all to myself.'

The eyes that locked with hers held so much sincerity and love her doubts evaporated. For how long she didn't yet know, but she now knew that she could always discuss them with this wonderful man. He'd help her through. 'Go on, then.' At his astonished look, she laughed. 'That's a yes. I will marry you, Jackson. And love you for ever, as well as all those children. Jessica Wilson, here I come.'

This time his kiss wasn't so gentle. More like demanding as he sealed their promise. 'Thank goodness,' he sighed between their lips. 'Thought I'd be spending the next year trying to sweet-talk you into a wedding.'

When Jackson drove up to his parents' house Nicholas was waiting on the veranda. He immediately began waving and leaping up and down.

'Mummy, I've been watching for you for ages.'

Her heart squeezed painfully. Her boy. She loved him beyond reason. Reaching to lift him into her arms, panic struck and she spun around to stare at Jackson.

'No, Jess, you haven't neglected him for other people. You were doing your job and now you're home to hug and hold and love your son. That's normal for most parents.' Jackson stood beside her, lifting strands of hair off her face.

'Thank you.' She sucked in the sweet smell of Nicholas as he wriggled around in her arms. She felt his warmth warming her. Knew he'd always come first with her.

'Mummy, there was a very big eel in the packing shed. Ian said the flood brought it here. I touched it and it was cold and yucky.'

Jackson took her elbow and led them inside. 'Let's get changed into something clean and warm and I'll break out the champagne. We've got something to celebrate.'

Her mouth stretched so wide it hurt. 'Yeah. We do. But first I need some time with Nicholas. I've got something to discuss with him.'

Jackson nodded his understanding. 'Why don't you go through to Mum's office? I'll make sure no one disturbs you.'

In the office she sat in the one comfortable chair and settled Nicholas on her lap. 'We're going to live in a different house for a while, Nicholas. Our one was flooded.'

His little eyes widened with something like excitement. 'Really? Can I see it with the water in it?'

How easy things were for a child. 'We'll go there tomorrow, but the water's gone now.'

Disappointment replaced the excitement. 'I wanted to see it.'

Drawing a deep breath, she continued with the other

important piece of news. 'Nicholas, how would you like Jackson to live with us? All the time?'

The excitement rushed back. 'Yes. When? Now?' His face fell. 'But he can't. We haven't got a house to live in.'

'We'll find another house. Mummy and Jackson are going to get married. You'll have a daddy.'

'Like Robby's daddy?' Hope radiated out of his big eyes.

Shame hit her. She'd held out on Jackson because she'd feared she'd be hurting her son, yet all along the best thing she could've done for him was accept Jackson's love and go with it. 'Just like Robby's father.'

She kissed her boy. 'I love you, Nicholas.'

'I love you, Mummy. I love Jackson.' He slid off her knees. 'Is he really, really going to be my daddy?'

'Yes, darling, he is.'

A whirlwind of arms and legs raced for the door, hauled it open and Nicholas took off to charge through the house. 'Where's my daddy? Jackson, where are you? Mummy and Jackson are getting married. Jackson? There you are.'

Jess made it to the door in time to see Jackson swinging Nicholas up in his arms, both of them grinning like loons.

'Guess everyone in the bay's going to know in no time at all.' She shook her head at Nicholas, her heart brimming with love. 'Quiet has never been one of your attributes, my boy.'

Jackson rolled his eyes. 'It's funny, but I'm happy if the whole world knows I'm marrying you.'

CHAPTER TWELVE

SIX MONTHS LATER, on a perfect spring day, with a sky
the colour of love, Jess walked down the path leading
through Virginia's garden to the marquee once again set
up on the Wilsons' front lawn. Jess clung to Ian's arm,
her fingers digging in hard as her high heels negotiated
the newly laid pebbles. 'Thank you for standing in for
my father,' she told Jackson's dad.

True to form, Mum and Dad hadn't been able to make
it home for the wedding. Something about the gorillas
in Borneo needing their attention. Jess swallowed her
disappointment. She was about to get a whole new family: one that would always be there for her, as she would
be for them.

'I'm thrilled you asked me.' Ian looked down at her
with tears in his eyes. 'I'm getting to be a dab hand at it.
Two weddings in less than a year. Who'd have believed
it? And before we reach that son of mine, who's looking
mighty pleased with himself, can I just say thank you for
bringing him home for us.'

'Thank goodness he didn't have long to go to finish
his contract.' She'd have gone crazy if he'd been away
much longer than the four months he'd had to do. Now
he worked three days a week in Nelson and the rest of the
time at the Golden Bay Medical and Wellbeing Centre.

Sasha spoke behind them. 'Come on, you two. We've got a wedding to get under way, and Nicholas and I can't stand around all afternoon listening to you both yabbering.'

Jess turned and grinned at her soon-to-be sister-in-law. 'Yes, ma'am. By the way, you looked lovely in blue.'

'Why do my friends get married when I'm looking like a house in a dress?' For the second time Sasha was standing up for a close friend while pregnant.

Jess grinned and glanced down at Nicholas. He looked gorgeous in his dove-grey suit and sky-blue shirt that matched Jackson and Grady's. 'Let's get the show under way. What do you reckon, Nicholas?'

'Hurry up, Mummy. It's boring standing here.'

Jess grinned. 'Love you too, buddy.' Then she faced the end of the path, where Jackson stood watching her take every step along that path. When she placed her hand on his arm he blinked back tears. 'You are beautiful,' he murmured. His eyes glittered with emotion.

She couldn't say a word for the lump clogging her throat, so she reached up and kissed him lightly.

'Seems we need to get you two married in a hurry.' Diane, the marriage celebrant, chuckled. She looked around at the family and friends gathered on the lawn. 'Jessica and Jackson stand here today in front of you all to pledge themselves to each other.'

Jess heard the words and yet they ran over her like warm oil, soft and soothing. Not once on that day in January, when she'd stood up with Jackson, watching her best friend marry Grady, had it occurred to her that she'd be getting married in this same place, with the same people surrounding them. She hadn't known love like it—the depth, the generosity, the bone-melting sweetness. She hadn't known the colour of love—summer blue with sunshine lightening it. Okay, today it was spring blue, but that was close enough.

In fact, it was brilliant, as Jackson said the vows he'd written himself, declaring his love for her, promising her so much. Her heart squeezed tight with love. This wonderful man was becoming her husband. Handing Sasha her bouquet, she held her hands out to him. The diamond-encrusted wedding ring he slipped onto her finger gleamed in the sunlight.

'Jess, would you say your vows now.' Diane caught her attention.

Taking Jackson's strong, warm hands back in hers, she managed a strong voice. 'Jackson Wilson, today I promise before our family and friends to always love you with all my heart, to share my life with you, to raise our children alongside you. I acknowledge you as my son's father in the truest sense of the word. I love you. We love you.' And then she couldn't say any more for the tears in Jackson's eyes and the lump in her throat.

Sasha placed the gold band she and Jackson had chosen into her shaking hand. Her fingers trembled so much Jackson had to help her slide the ring up his finger. And then he kissed her. Thoroughly. No chaste wedding kiss.

'Okay, that's enough, you two,' Ian interrupted. 'There are children present,' he added, with a twinkle in his eye.

Diane smiled. 'I declare you man and wife.'

'Good, then I can kiss the bride,' Jackson said.

There was a general groan and many quips from the people seated around them, but none of it stopped Jackson placing his lips on hers again.

Once more Ian interrupted by pulling her out of his son's arms into his. 'Welcome to the family, Jessica.'

Then Virginia and Sasha were hugging her, quickly

followed by Nicholas, Grady, Mike and Roz, Rory and Mrs Harrop. Time sped by until Ian tapped a glass with a spoon and got everyone's attention.

'Champagne is being brought around. Let's all raise a glass and drink to Jessica and Jackson.'

Champagne. That's where this had all started. Her smile was met by one from her husband. 'Yep, it's the same champagne.'

As they were handed glasses of her favourite nectar, Jess grinned. 'I won't be drinking as much of this as I did the last time. I want all my faculties working on my wedding night.'

Jackson ran his hand through his hair, instantly mussing it up. 'I seem to remember they worked fine that other time.'

He slipped his free hand through her arm and tugged her away from the crowd and through the rose garden that was Ian's latest hobby. 'I want a few moments alone with my wife.'

'You sound very smug, Mr Wilson.'

'Why wouldn't I? I've just achieved a dream. You look absolutely beautiful. That dress with the orange flowers suits you to perfection.'

'Apricot, not orange.' She leaned against him and pressed a kiss to his mouth. 'I love you.'

For a moment they were completely alone. No voices touched their seclusion and nothing interrupted the sense that they were in their own little world. Then Jackson pulled his mouth free. 'I hope you've packed that orange bikini for our honeymoon.'

She'd done what she'd been told to do. Jackson had kept their destination a surprise, only saying that she'd need bikinis, lots of them. 'Of course.' And two other new ones he hadn't seen yet. Not apricot in colour, either of them.

'Our flight to Auckland leaves tomorrow afternoon.'

'Right.' Like she'd be wearing a bikini in Auckland in spring.

'Then on Monday we fly to Fiji.' That smug look just got smugger.

Secretly she'd hoped that's where he'd chosen. 'Fiji?' She grinned. 'You remembered.' Her kiss smothered his chuckle.

'We're away for two weeks, sweetheart.'

'Our house will be finished by then.' There was only the paintwork to be completed and the carpet to be put down in their new home before they were handed the keys.

'That will make you happy. Being back on your piece of dirt where you planned on bringing up Nicholas.'

That was one of the things she loved about this man. He understood her need to put down roots for herself, and how she had done that when she'd bought her little home. Which was why, when the insurance company had elected to bowl over both her houses and pay out the money, they'd had the two sections made into one and started building a house big enough to cope with the children they intended on having very soon.

'Mummy, Jackson, come on. Everyone's hungry and we're not allowed to eat until you sit at your table.' Nicholas burst through the bushes they'd hidden behind. 'Come on.'

'That means you're the hungry one.' Jackson swung his son up into his arms, and nudged Jess softly. 'Guess we'd better return to our wedding.'

She followed her men back to the front lawn and into the marquee, decorated in apricot and sky blue: the colour of love.

* * *

As they sat down at the top table Jackson pinched himself. It had happened. He'd married his love. His beautiful Jessica. She'd changed him, saved him really. Shown him that the important things in life were family, community, generosity. She'd brought him to his senses. But most of all she'd shown him love.

'Didn't I tell you it was time for you to return home?' Ping stood in front of them, nodding sagely.

Standing, Jackson reached over to shake the hand of his best buddy. 'Yes, Ping, you did. Took me a while to hear what you were saying.'

'Jessica's a good woman, that's for sure.' Ping draped an arm over the shoulders of the petite woman standing beside him. 'Like my Chen.'

Chen smiled and elbowed her husband. 'You're talking too much again, husband.'

Ping laughed. 'I can see why this Golden Bay brought you back. It's beautiful. All that land with only cattle on it. And the sea that's so clean.'

'You'll be moving here next,' Jackson told him.

Ping and Chen shook their heads at the same time. 'We've got family that we'd never leave back in Hong Kong. More important than green paddocks and sparkling waters.'

Exactly. Family. There was nothing more important. So important that he would soon quit his days in Nelson and become a full-time partner in the medical centre in town. There was no way he'd be leaving Jess and Nicholas for three days at a time every week. Absolutely no way.

Beside him Jess was talking and laughing with Sasha, as happy as he'd ever seen her. Her eyes were fudge-coloured today, matching that orange ribbon wound through her fair hair. A lump blocked the air to his lungs. He'd do anything for this woman who'd stolen his heart. Blinking rapidly, he looked around the marquee at all their friends and family, here to celebrate with them.

Lifting his eyes, he noted the decorations. Blue and orange ribbons festooned the walls. Orange. He grinned as he heard Jess growling, *It's apricot.* Apricot, orange. Whatever. For him, this was the colour of love.

* * * * *

Mills & Boon® Hardback
June 2014

ROMANCE

Ravelli's Defiant Bride	Lynne Graham
When Da Silva Breaks the Rules	Abby Green
The Heartbreaker Prince	Kim Lawrence
The Man She Can't Forget	Maggie Cox
A Question of Honour	Kate Walker
What the Greek Can't Resist	Maya Blake
An Heir to Bind Them	Dani Collins
Playboy's Lesson	Melanie Milburne
Don't Tell the Wedding Planner	Aimee Carson
The Best Man for the Job	Lucy King
Falling for Her Rival	Jackie Braun
More than a Fling?	Joss Wood
Becoming the Prince's Wife	Rebecca Winters
Nine Months to Change His Life	Marion Lennox
Taming Her Italian Boss	Fiona Harper
Summer with the Millionaire	Jessica Gilmore
Back in Her Husband's Arms	Susanne Hampton
Wedding at Sunday Creek	Leah Martyn

MEDICAL

200 Harley Street: The Soldier Prince	Kate Hardy
200 Harley Street: The Enigmatic Surgeon	Annie Claydon
A Father for Her Baby	Sue MacKay
The Midwife's Son	Sue MacKay

0514GEN STD HB

Mills & Boon® Large Print

June 2014

ROMANCE

A Bargain with the Enemy	Carole Mortimer
A Secret Until Now	Kim Lawrence
Shamed in the Sands	Sharon Kendrick
Seduction Never Lies	Sara Craven
When Falcone's World Stops Turning	Abby Green
Securing the Greek's Legacy	Julia James
An Exquisite Challenge	Jennifer Hayward
Trouble on Her Doorstep	Nina Harrington
Heiress on the Run	Sophie Pembroke
The Summer They Never Forgot	Kandy Shepherd
Daring to Trust the Boss	Susan Meier

HISTORICAL

Portrait of a Scandal	Annie Burrows
Drawn to Lord Ravenscar	Anne Herries
Lady Beneath the Veil	Sarah Mallory
To Tempt a Viking	Michelle Willingham
Mistress Masquerade	Juliet Landon

MEDICAL

From Venice with Love	Alison Roberts
Christmas with Her Ex	Fiona McArthur
After the Christmas Party...	Janice Lynn
Her Mistletoe Wish	Lucy Clark
Date with a Surgeon Prince	Meredith Webber
Once Upon a Christmas Night...	Annie Claydon

Mills & Boon® Hardback

July 2014

ROMANCE

Christakis's Rebellious Wife	Lynne Graham
At No Man's Command	Melanie Milburne
Carrying the Sheikh's Heir	Lynn Raye Harris
Bound by the Italian's Contract	Janette Kenny
Dante's Unexpected Legacy	Catherine George
A Deal with Demakis	Tara Pammi
The Ultimate Playboy	Maya Blake
Socialite's Gamble	Michelle Conder
Her Hottest Summer Yet	Ally Blake
Who's Afraid of the Big Bad Boss?	Nina Harrington
If Only...	Tanya Wright
Only the Brave Try Ballet	Stefanie London
Her Irresistible Protector	Michelle Douglas
The Maverick Millionaire	Alison Roberts
The Return of the Rebel	Jennifer Faye
The Tycoon and the Wedding Planner	Kandy Shepherd
The Accidental Daddy	Meredith Webber
Pregnant with the Soldier's Son	Amy Ruttan

MEDICAL

200 Harley Street: The Shameless Maverick	Louisa George
200 Harley Street: The Tortured Hero	Amy Andrews
A Home for the Hot-Shot Doc	Dianne Drake
A Doctor's Confession	Dianne Drake

Mills & Boon® Large Print

July 2014

ROMANCE

A Prize Beyond Jewels	Carole Mortimer
A Queen for the Taking?	Kate Hewitt
Pretender to the Throne	Maisey Yates
An Exception to His Rule	Lindsay Armstrong
The Sheikh's Last Seduction	Jennie Lucas
Enthralled by Moretti	Cathy Williams
The Woman Sent to Tame Him	Victoria Parker
The Plus-One Agreement	Charlotte Phillips
Awakened By His Touch	Nikki Logan
Road Trip with the Eligible Bachelor	Michelle Douglas
Safe in the Tycoon's Arms	Jennifer Faye

HISTORICAL

The Fall of a Saint	Christine Merrill
At the Highwayman's Pleasure	Sarah Mallory
Mishap Marriage	Helen Dickson
Secrets at Court	Blythe Gifford
The Rebel Captain's Royalist Bride	Anne Herries

MEDICAL

Her Hard to Resist Husband	Tina Beckett
The Rebel Doc Who Stole Her Heart	Susan Carlisle
From Duty to Daddy	Sue MacKay
Changed by His Son's Smile	Robin Gianna
Mr Right All Along	Jennifer Taylor
Her Miracle Twins	Margaret Barker

Discover more romance at

www.millsandboon.co.uk

- ❤ WIN great prizes in our exclusive competitions
- ❤ BUY new titles before they hit the shops
- ❤ BROWSE new books and REVIEW your favourites
- ❤ SAVE on new books with the Mills & Boon® Bookclub™
- ❤ DISCOVER new authors

PLUS, to chat about your favourite reads, get the latest news and find special offers:

- Find us on facebook.com/millsandboon
- Follow us on twitter.com/millsandboonuk
- ❤ Sign up to our newsletter at millsandboon.co.uk